CRAFTING A KNOCKOFF

Gasper's Cove Mysteries Book 7

BARBARA EMODI

Publisher: Amy Barrett-Daffin

Creative Director: Gailen Runge

Senior Editor: Roxane Cerda

Copy Editor: Second Glance Editorial

Cover Designer: Mariah Sinclair

Book Designer: April Mostek

Production Coordinator: Zinnia Heinzmann

Illustrator: Emilija Mihajlov

Published by C&T Publishing, Inc., P.O. Box 1456, Lafayette, CA 94549

Library of Congress Control Number: 2026931379

Printed in the USA

10 9 8 7 6 5 4 3 2 1

Gasper's Cove Mysteries Series

• *Book 1* •
Crafting for Murder

• *Book 2* •
Crafting Deception

• *Book 3* •
Crafting with Slander

• *Book 4* •
Crafting a Getaway

• *Book 5* •
Crafting an Alibi

• *Book 6* •
Crafting a Cold Case

• *Book 7* •
Crafting a Knockoff

DEDICATION

Allan MacDonald. For his electrical expertise and, more importantly, for his deep understanding of character and culture—a bright light in our family.

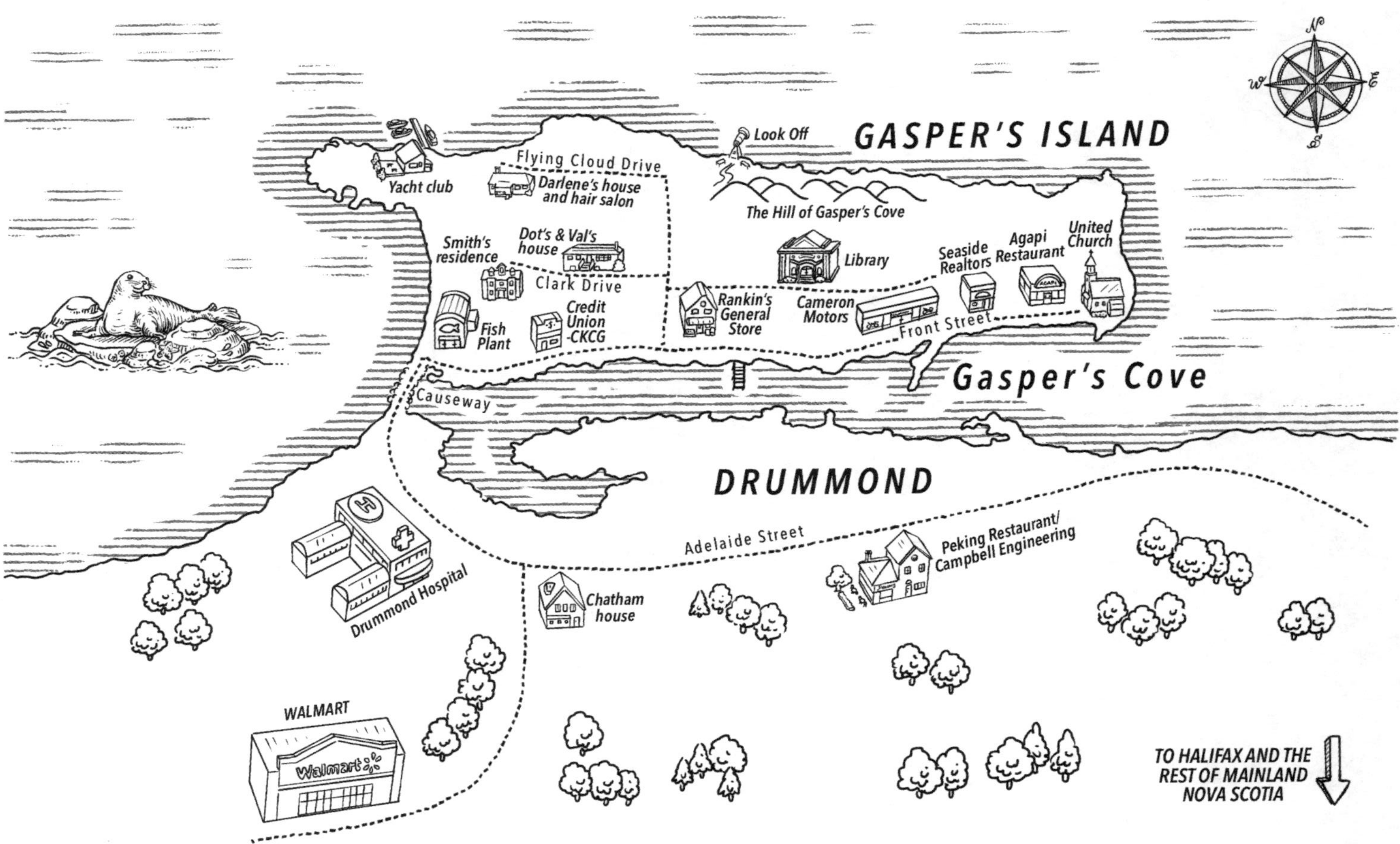
N
E
S
W
GASPER'S ISLAND
Look Off
Flying Cloud Drive
Yacht club
Darlene's house and hair salon
The Hill of Gasper's Cove
Smith's residence
Dot's & Val's house
Clark Drive
Library
Seaside Realtors
Agapi Restaurant
United Church
Fish Plant
Credit Union -CKCG
Rankin's General Store
Cameron Motors
Front Street
Gasper's Cove
Causeway
DRUMMOND
Adelaide Street
Peking Restaurant/ Campbell Engineering
Drummond Hospital
Chatham house
WALMART
Walmart
TO HALIFAX AND THE REST OF MAINLAND NOVA SCOTIA

CHAPTER ONE

Craft shows can be dangerous.

Deadly.

I should know.

The signs told me to stay safe at home.

Dark clouds pressed down on the street outside, promising nothing good. One shoe had disappeared overnight. While I looked for it, I spilled my coffee on the outfit I had made for this day, a silk jersey I couldn't afford—dry clean only, now ruined. I changed into my backup, a rayon dress everyone had seen before, and that made me look matronly. Toby, my golden retriever rescue, positioned himself between me and the door. I tried to reassure him and reached for my keys on the little vestibule table where they rested between drives. Where had they gone? Run off with the shoe?

Oh, the warnings were there. Whispering to me like they sometimes did.

Did I pay attention?

Of course not.

How could I? This was the end of May, the last chance to sell winter-made crafts before the first full moon in June, the official start of the Nova Scotia gardening season, which would consume everyone's weekends. The importance of the Thirteenth Annual Gasper's Cove Spring Craft Show overrode any distractions or omens. My cousin Darlene would be at the booth in the arena now, waiting for me.

But how would I get there? Where were my keys?

I searched. First in logical places, like pockets, then in illogical ones, like behind the 40-year-old smocked cushions inherited with the house from my aunt. I even looked under the whisk and wooden spoons in a kitchen drawer. I gave up. In my experience, lost things were found when *they* were ready.

It couldn't be rushed.

Until then, I had an emergency. I had one option left. I took it.

I called Stuart.

"Are you out and about?" I asked casually, as if I were passing the time. Stuart was a friend, and one I thought about more than I liked to admit. I didn't want it to be too obvious that he was also evolving into my Mr. Reliable. "In the car, maybe?"

"I'm on my way to the yacht club for a meeting." There was a pause while Stuart listened for what I hadn't said. "You can't find your car keys again." This was a statement, not a question. "Where do you want to go?"

The yacht club was at one end of the island, the arena at the other.

"Nowhere," I lied. "I'm fine."

"The show. It's today, isn't it? Wait for me in front of the house. I'm turning around."

Stuart hung up before I could say, "Don't bother." Or "Thank you."

Gasper's Cove arena hosted craft shows every spring and fall. In small Nova Scotian communities, hockey rinks are often used for any gathering too large for a living room or a church basement.

The arena was not a perfect venue. Cold and drafty, its disguise as an exhibition hall was questionable, but it was big enough to hold the throngs of shoppers, craftspeople, and retailers who poured in from the local area, the rest of the province, and even New England. For many artisans, sales from the shows were a major source of income. This mattered. Traditionally, forestry and fishing had dominated Nova Scotia's economy. But recently, tourism, with its appetite for crafts, was catching up. The Gasper's Cove Crafter's Co-op had a booth at both the pre-Christmas show and this one, marking the end of winter. The spring event was my favorite. To me, the rows of tables displaying what creative people had made over the cold, dark months were as much a confirmation of the persistence of life as the spring tulips.

It didn't take Stuart long to pick me up and get me to the rink. The old building was nestled like a giant weathered turtle at the end of Front Street, not far from our family store, Rankin's General Store, on the side of the road away from the water, and near where the remnants of the town petered out. Stuart knew his way around the arena's parking lot. He bypassed the big public doors out front and drove me straight up to the exhibiter's entrance at the back of the building. He parked near the loading-dock doors, next to a diagonal row of panel vans, one with Sparky's Electrical painted on its side.

"Looks like Jimmy's working today," Stuart said, noticing the truck. "I hope Sparky's paying him overtime."

"Don't count on it," I said, then regretted it. Sparky Bailey was the only electrical contractor in town. He ran his business with the combination of nonchalance and greed that monopolies tended to encourage. I suspected that Sparky paid his employees just enough to make them show up at work, and not much more. Jimmy MacNeil, Stuart's favorite nephew, was Sparky's best young electrician. I knew Stuart worried about Jimmy, his sister's son. He didn't need me to confirm that Jimmy could have done better than settle for a future with the local contractor.

Stuart sighed. "Jimmy needs to stand up for himself. I can't do it for him." He looked over at the box of pottery mugs on my lap. "Why don't I give you a hand taking those in?"

I considered the offer, and Stuart. He had on his new windbreaker with "President" embroidered over the yacht club logo. His dark curly hair was still damp from the shower, and he had even tried to part it. I had diverted him on his way to his first meeting as the club's new president. Stuart was never late for anything. He shouldn't be late for this. Not because of me.

"No. You go." I hoisted the load of mugs myself and got out of the car before Stuart could help me. "I've got Darlene in there. She'll help me unpack."

"I don't know, Valerie," Stuart said, doubtfully, "that box looks heavy."

"Go. I'll be fine." I got out of the car and closed the door on his protests.

Stuart hesitated, then drove away, his tires crunching on the gravel, his eyes on me in the rearview mirror.

The box weighed more than I had admitted. I shifted it to one hip to free up a hand to pull open the metal door to the arena. The door, weary, dented, and battered by decades of hockey sticks and boys horsing around, protested. I noted a paper sign—"Authorized Exhibitors Only!"—taped over "Player's Entrance." I knew the arena would be hockey-chilly inside, despite the flooring laid over the ice and the bunting and promotional banners draped over the rink's boards to hide the penalty boxes.

Stepping through the doorway was like walking into a freezer. Inside, I adjusted my box, pushed my handbag farther up my shoulder, and moved across the landing to the steep concrete steps down to the center of the arena, where it would be warmer once the crowds showed up. Behind me, the door opened, then shut, with finality. Other exhibitors, with their own loads, lined up around me. First in line, and conscious of them, I moved forward to the stairwell.

I lifted my foot. It skidded on the wet tread of the first step.

I tried to shift my box again so I could grab the handrail.

But before I could find it, there was a loud crack overhead.

The lights went out.

I stopped still, my foot raised. The steps in front of me disappeared.

The box loosened in my arms. The weight of the pottery inside pulled me forward.

I wobbled.

Someone rushed down the stairs past me. Instead of offering the helping hand I expected, they shoved me into the wall. I caught the smell of mothballs and thought of wool. Distracted, I felt my balance go. My shoes slipped.

I fell, throwing my collection of hand-turned coffee mugs ahead of me. I heard them bounce down the stairs, smashing as they went, ricocheting down over the concrete steps. One last time, I tried to find the handrail. It had vanished. My fingers skidded over the painted blocks of the wall. Out of control, I covered my face with my arms, as I fell faster than I could think. Instinctively, I braced myself, closed my eyes tight, and waited for a messy end, smashed into the concrete floor of a converted ice rink.

Instead, I made a soft landing into a pile of ...

Quilts.

The lights went on.

I was stretched out full length, belly down, surrounded by broken pottery, but safe. Unhurt. I lifted my head to get a better look at what had broken my fall. I had, by some miracle, by the intervention of some angel who knew how to sew, landed not on a hard, unwelcoming arena floor but onto a trolley stacked with quilts. The one under me I recognized immediately as a double wedding ring, hand-stitched and meticulously pieced. Reflexively, I smoothed the fabric. Judging by the wear and the small motifs of the fabric, it had been made in the 1950s or earlier, maybe in the 1940s. Some of the fabric in the borders looked like feed-sack cotton. The handiwork and intervention of other women in another time had saved me.

My world made sense again.

I sat up.

A firm grip helped me to my feet.

"My quilts!" A tall blond woman in a crazy quilt jacket inspected my landing place through turquoise framed glasses. "Good," she muttered to herself, "no blood." She flashed me a smile and flared her eyelash extensions. "And you? Are you alright?"

"Fine," I said, looking at the shattered mugs on the concrete floor. "Better than my pottery. When the lights went out, I guess I tripped."

The woman looked up into the arena's rafters. She was annoyed but trying to be gracious, even though she didn't have the time for it.

"The electrical system in this building is a disgrace. This is the third time this morning this has happened. A decent show brings in outside power. All we have here is some kid who doesn't talk. But then again, where am I?"

"Gasper's Cove, Nova Scotia?" I offered. It was my turn to be gracious. My mother had brought me up to be polite to strangers, even rude ones.

"Right. 'Last Gasp' they called it at the hotel over in Drummond." She waited for me to laugh along with her. "That's funny," she explained.

I looked down at the wedding ring at my feet. The hand quilting was impeccable, every stitch regular, undoubtedly done years ago by a fisherman's wife during long, lonely, worried evenings.

"Beautiful work," I said. I felt it was time to talk about what locals did, not where we were. "Are you a collector? Here to sell?"

The woman held out her dolman-sleeved arms for inspection. She was thin under the colorful padded jacket and dressed all in black. She wore a turtleneck, a long narrow skirt, and high-heeled boots with toes so pointed, they would be useful for stepping on spiders in corners.

"Louise Haggerty," she announced, as if her name explained everything. I searched my memory for information on any Haggertys I knew and came up blank. "The designer," she elaborated. "Montreal. Toronto. New York. Palm Beach?"

So many cities? My first thought was that the Haggertys must be a big family, then I caught myself.

"Designer?" I asked. "You mean clothes? I sew too. I teach classes." We had something in common. I'd work with that.

Louise lowered her arms, possibly in defeat.

"Sustainable fashion. We upcycle original textiles into unique pieces. No two are the same. I collect hand-embroidered linens and quilts." She looked down at the trolley at her feet. "I let the pieces inspire me. I usually don't do these shows myself." She exhaled all her second thoughts. "But my marketing man suggested I come up here. I thought, why not? I am always looking for sources. Like the ones you fell on."

Louise Haggerty had my attention. These quilts were from here? Who from? I wondered. Homes up and down the shore all had quilts like these. I'd be interested to know who was selling. I'd find that out. Not much got past my crafting network.

"Sorry," I said, putting out my hand. "Valerie Rankin. I'm here with the Crafter's Co-Op. We have a booth."

"Ahh, I've heard of you," Louise let her hand float over mine without touching it. "You manage that store, don't you? Rankin's General? You run a crafter's thingy out of the second floor, am I right?"

"That's me. If we make it, we sell it. Got a great bunch of knitters, carvers, quilters ... "

"Right," Louise cut me off. "That's why my guy must have you in his export-focused sights. He said as much. Murray Nunn. Wider markets are where the real money is. But speak to me before you sign anything."

Sign what? What was this woman she talking about? I had just fallen down a flight of stairs in a hockey arena. I had broken some of my best merchandise. I was wearing my second-best outfit. Somewhere inside this arena, I had a cousin in a craft booth looking at her watch and wondering where I was. I had passed my capacity for excitement and new information somewhere down along the seventh or eighth step. I had real things to do.

"Great to meet you," I said as politely as I could, while I moved toward the double doors into the exhibit hall. "I'll be sure to drop by and see your clothes. I have a lot to set up. I've got to get to my booth." Show staff had arrived and were sweeping up the shards of broken mugs.

Louise slapped her hands on the handle of the trolley and moved past me. She seemed determined to do her best to use it like a quilt-stacked battering ram to get through the crowd and closer to the door.

"Brilliant," she said. "Let's catch up when we can. Grab a coffee." The other exhibitors parted to let her by. "Never risk competition when you can choose collaboration," she tossed back.

I watched Louise disappear into the show.

That sounded to me like good advice.

Or maybe another warning.

I wasn't sure which.

CHAPTER TWO

Darlene rushed to meet me. On her way, her coral heel caught on the extension cord taped to the floor of our booth, number 13. She fired questions at me while she pulled her shoe free.

"Where have you been? Where's your new outfit? Why that dress? Why didn't you call me?" My cousin stopped and looked at my empty arms. "And where's the pottery? Did you forget it?"

"I didn't forget the mugs. They are in the recycling bin in the back stairwell." I put my bag under a draped table covered with quilted place mats and knitted baby clothes. "When the lights went out, I fell and dropped the box. Nothing's left. I don't know how to tell the Mudslingers. I feel terrible. They worked so hard to get ready for this weekend."

"Don't worry about them. You can't take everything on." Darlene dismissed my concern. "You know what potters are like. They'll write it off to karma and make some more. The main thing is, are you hurt?"

"No, I'm fine. A pile of quilts from that woman over there saved me." I pointed across to where Louise had arrived in Booths 16 and 18, with a sizable, professionally painted sign suspended above that read "Re-Creations: Sustainable Wearable Art."

"That's all that matters." Darlene patted my arm and then lifted hers to wave to someone she knew in the passing stream of other vendors. As the town's former, and best, hair stylist and its current deputy mayor, Darlene was on waving terms with all of Gasper's Cove. "What do you think of the neighborhood? We're in dinky spots on the small-business side of the aisle, and the big-time operators over there got the doubles."

Darlene was right. Our booth was on the edge of the rink, next to a screen attempting to conceal the visiting players' bench, between Booth 11, Terry's Tartans, and Booth 15, Nancy's Novelties. Across the way, in the center of the show floor, flanking Re-Creations: Sustainable Wearable Art, was The Salt Box: Nouvelle New Scotland Cuisine, in Booths 12 and 14, and the show's information and media center in Booths 20 and 22.

"I talked to her, you know. The quilted-clothing lady," I said, moving aside in our small space to make room for Nancy Mullins from next door. "On my way in, at the bottom of the stairs. She was right where I landed."

The three of us turned to watch the designer bustle around her booth with a clothes steamer. Her quilted, refashioned, wearable-art jacket looked stiff and uneasy on the trim, chic form underneath it.

Nancy, petite and round, surveyed the other exhibitor with interest over the top of her wire-framed glasses, her blue eyes accented with a not-unsubstantial quantity of aquamarine eye shadow. "What's she like, then?" she asked.

"Nice," I said, lost for a way to accurately describe the designer. "Businesslike, in a not-from-around-here way. Her name is Louise, and she has her own marketing consultant." This last fact impressed me, although I didn't know why. "That must mean she's doing well. But there was something funny about how she talked about this consultant. I don't think she really trusts him. She told me to be careful if he tries to talent-scout us."

"Talent scout? Us?" Nancy leaned in for more information and, hopefully, gossip. She had different earrings in each ear, one silver and one gold. I wondered if this reflected a rushed morning or if it was another display of Nancy's taste for novelty. "Who is this guy?"

"Murray Nunn. I know him," Darlene interrupted. She moved closer to share exclusive intelligence. "He was at the last council meeting. He gave us a pitch about his results-focused expertise, as he calls it, in economic development. He wants us to connect him with local businesses." She looked over at Louise, who had put the steamer down to talk to a man with a video camera. "The quilted-jacket woman might be right about his trying to recruit you. Nunn asked about the Co-op. He said he had a special interest in *cultural industries*."

"Cultural? Like sewing? Quilting? Knitting? Crochet?" I asked. "Painters? Artists?"

"Probably," Darlene conceded. "Mind you, I did some checking up on him. As far as I can tell, up to now, all he's done is help small manufacturers access government development money. My guess is that he's a standard-issue middleman who knows how to work the system to access funding. His clients have been outfits that make fishing gear, plastic boxes for lobster, navigational software, modular lawn furniture, and parts for windmills. Mostly boring, technical stuff. I don't know how he would do promoting a craft business. I doubt if he'd know the difference between mass production and handmade."

A gaggle of other exhibitors walked into the booths across from us. Louise held up a Dresden Plate vest and a long coat made of faded Log Cabin blocks for them to gush over.

"Mass production? How does he do that with her?" I asked Darlene. "She's selling recycled vintage garments. One-of-a-kinds."

"That's what she says, but let's be real. Surely the genuine artists were whoever did the original embroidery or made the quilts in the first place," Darlene said. "Anyone can get them cut up and restitched. The way I see it, she's not a designer as much as a repackager."

"You got that right," Nancy chimed in. She had information of her own to share. "I know someone whose niece was in her store in New York. Old Louise sells her vests for $1,000 and her jackets for nearly $3,000! Can you imagine?"

"Get out, I don't believe you." As someone who made all her own clothes, this shocked me.

"Believe it. And most of that's profit," Nancy continued. "I never miss an estate sale, and let me tell you, lately she's been at them all. She even wanted to buy from me, but I wouldn't sell, not the quilts. That would be a sin. Too much work went into them. Some of those quilts were made as wedding presents." Nancy's eyes misted under her blue lids. She sniffed and pulled a handkerchief with a tatted edging from her sleeve. "I'd never let a love story get cut up. Not with my family background, I wouldn't."

Nancy paused to let her gaze linger on the large diamond on Darlene's left hand, snug against my cousin's new wedding band. Darlene had recently, and finally, married her high school sweetheart, George Kosoulas. Nancy, one in the long line of legendary Mullins matchmakers, had not been involved in their romance but liked to say she couldn't have organized a better union herself.

I was the only single woman in our booth. Nancy returned her damp handkerchief to her sleeve and smiled at me. I tucked both my hands into the pockets of my dress. My status as a middle-aged, long divorced woman with three grown children worried her. I knew a question about Stuart was on its way.

I headed her off.

"Darlene? What did the council say to this Mr. Nunn?"

"What we say to all the consultants, real estate developers, and so-called entrepreneurs," Darlene shrugged. "We voted to ask for more information, a proposal, or plan in writing. A request for details usually means we'll never see them again. We have to do it. The mayor gets overexcited when he hears about any chance to extend the tax base. The rest of us have to keep him under control."

Darlene stopped talking to gesture across the aisle to the two men who had arrived at the Salt Box booth. The one in a shiny blue suit (polyester, not silk, I could tell that from twenty feet away) was speaking into a small headset. The other man, the same one I'd seen in conversation with Louise, stood a short distance away, filming.

"That's Murray Nunn over there now, with his videographer," Darlene said. "They're making some kind of promotional video for Moira's restaurant. Why don't you go over and introduce yourself, Val?"

"Maybe later," I said. I was too rattled by my fall to talk to strangers.

"Go," Nancy urged. "While Moira is still handing out samples of shortbread. It's some good. She says it's from an old recipe her ancestors, the Frasers, brought over on the *Hector*."

"The *Hector?* Are you sure?" The *Hector* was Nova Scotia's version of the *Mayflower* and had arrived in Pictou County from Scotland in 1773 with only 200 passengers, half of them small children. "That's some old recipe," I said.

"Yes, not a word of a lie," Nancy assured me. "That's how Moira's making a name for herself. She's calling it 'heritage cuisine.' Taking the past and putting it on a plate. Mind you, that's safer now since the invention of refrigeration." Nancy giggled. She enjoyed making people laugh almost as much as she liked marrying them off.

"The Salt Box is a beautiful place for dinner," Darlene pointed out. "But expensive. George took me there for my birthday. It takes a lot to impress a guy who runs a Greek restaurant, but he liked it. Lots of atmosphere. The old recipe book is in a glass case at the front. And there is even tartan the family brought over from the old country framed on the wall. Romantic. You and Stuart should go, Val."

Nancy snapped to attention at the mention of Stuart's name and slid closer to my side, in case I divulged any matrimonially useful information. I looked around the arena for a conversational exit.

"Speaking of tartan, how's Terry doing?" I asked. The booth beside us was a riot of plaid—kilts on unstable mannequins, stacks of hats, scarves, blankets, and capes piled high on portable, folding tables of the Canadian Tire kind. It was as if Terry Mowat were expecting a retail onslaught of the Gathering of the Clans. On one table, in a basket, I spotted pairs of clan tartan oven mitts, in another, a display of family tartan dog collars.

"Terry's the same," Darlene said. "That plaid is an excuse to chat. A retired provincial archivist is the best man to talk to if you know your last name and have time to fill. Even if he sells nothing, he'll be happy as a clam this weekend if he can spend two days straight discussing family trees. He's just back from a visit to Edinburgh, so he's fully recharged. But he knows his stuff. I heard he did some genealogy for Moira. She wanted it for branding."

The idea of family as a brand was new to me. But before I could ask Darlene to elaborate, the man with the video camera walked over to us.

"Ladies? I'm Jeff Robichaud. We're shooting across the way. Do you mind if I stand in your booth to take a shot?"

I studied the bulky unit on the videographer's shoulder. It was the size of an old all-metal sewing machine and probably just as heavy. But it looked to me as if Jeff was more than fit enough to handle it. He was a nice-looking fellow, probably still in his late thirties, and hip. His jeans had the creases of denim never washed. His "East Coast Living" T-shirt sleeves strained over gym-made biceps, and he had a neat bun, samurai-style, on top of his head.

"Be our guest," Darlene answered, fluffing up her hair and adjusting the name tag on her jacket. "Where do you want us to stand?"

"Behind me, if you wouldn't mind, out of the shot," Jeff suggested. "I want to pan over the show and get in the Salt Box's whole display. I need to be over here to do it."

"Will do," Darlene said, herding Nancy and me away closer to a rack of hand-woven ponchos. "I see you're working with Murray Nunn," she said to Jeff, smoothing away any evidence of her expectation that we were going to be filmed.

"That I am," Jeff replied, his back to us now, his eye pressed hard into the lens of his big camera while he twisted the focus. Satisfied he had set up the shot he wanted, he pulled his head back, looked up and down the aisle, and then smiled at us. "Looks like Murray's gone off somewhere. Shouldn't be far. Do you want to talk to him?"

"No, I'm good," I said. I had already made my mind up about a man I hadn't yet met. "It can wait."

No one knew the talent in Gasper's Cove better than I did. If there was any scouting to be done, if the Co-op was ever ready to grow, I, and not someone passing through, would be the one to do it.

CHAPTER THREE

Nancy, Darlene, and I moved to the back of the booth to watch Jeff work. He was agile and fast, moving around the tight space with choreographed precision as he stretched and twisted for the right angle. It was as if his body sensed what was around and behind him without looking. He bumped into nothing—not our sea-glass wind chimes, not our driftwood birds, not our tree of pewter earrings.

"Boy, what a pro," Nancy breathed in admiration. "I wonder if he does weddings."

"I doubt it," Darlene said. "I have his card. It says he does promotional work."

"Mm." Nancy thought this over. "I get it, more like engagements." She looked at her watch. "Listen. We have a few minutes before we have to start setting up. Valerie, why don't we run over and check out those quilted clothes while we have a chance?"

Nancy wasn't interested in investigating Louise's outerwear, and we both knew it. What she really wanted to explore was my relationship with Stuart, and to get me alone to talk. I didn't hold it against her. Nancy was under pressure. Online dating was affecting her operations. She needed a win to restore her reputation.

But I wasn't ready for it to be me.

"Drafty in here," I said, stalling. I dragged a merino cardigan from my bag.

"Hadn't noticed," Nancy said. She waited while I put the sweater on, adjusted the collar of my dress over the neckline, and rubbed hand lotion into my hands. She rolled her eyes at me and twisted her watch on her wrist, jingling the overloaded charm bracelet beside it. Four of the charms were gold-mounted baby teeth, one from each of her now middle-aged children. Nancy was a woman who did not let go easily.

I gave up.

"Alright," I said. "Let's go. Just the jackets. Quick."

Satisfied, Nancy pulled me across the aisle to the overflowing racks in Louise's booth. She reached into a rack at the front and pulled out a short crazy-quilt jacket, pieced from velvet and satin, seams covered in feathery embroidery in the Victorian style.

"Nice for going out in an evening," Nancy said, lifting her glasses for a better look. "Like a date. With a man. Are you going out much these days, Valerie? I mean, socially?"

I didn't answer. Nancy held the jacket up against me, like a mother outfitting a child for back-to-school, but in her case, happily-ever-after.

Mid-appraisal, Nancy stopped to look more closely at the garment in her hands.

"This is interesting," she whispered, glancing over at Louise. "She's used antique quilts, but in some places"—she lifted a sleeve—"where it shows less, there are new fabrics mixed in. A new block here and an old block there. She's watering it down, like soup in a diner. Bit sneaky." Nancy looked at the sign overhead, "Re-Creations? Is that what they call it?"

I leafed through the jackets out on the rack. Nancy was right. The undersides of collars, side panels, and the underarms of sleeves had reproduction fabrics worked in among the originals.

"It's everywhere," I said. I noticed something else. "Where are the price tags? You said she was charging a lot."

"That's what I was told. But"—Nancy leaned in to share a shopkeeper's insight—"I don't think she's here to sell. She's here to buy. And she doesn't want people to know how little she's paying them for the materials for her expensive 'designer' clothes. Get it?"

Before I could say that I did, the full clothing rack behind Nancy rolled aside, and Louise Haggerty stepped forward. I wondered if she'd heard our conversation, but if she had, Louise gave no sign.

That might have been because she wasn't alone. Behind Louise, near the cash table, was the man in the shiny blue suit. Murray Nunn caught my eye and smiled, at least the best he could, since his facial muscles didn't move. I made a quick assessment. The man himself was vintage, but also full of Botox. I knew the look. I'd studied the anchors on the TV news. Now, I wanted to meet Mr. Nunn, for a closer examination. Men with Botox were uncommon in Gasper's Cove.

"Ladies," Louise minced toward us. The feet in those spike-heel boots were going to hurt after a full ten-hour craft show day. "Can I help you?"

Nancy deftly jammed the crazy-quilt jacket back on the rod, next to an appliquéd vest. "No. We're just admiring your merchandise," she said, aquamarine-shadowed blue eyes wide and innocent.

Louise forced a smile. She didn't believe retailers checked out each other's wares unless they had an ulterior motive. She never would.

"Terrific," she said. "Any questions, let me know."

"Louise?" Murray Nunn asked, pushing his way into the conversation. "May I interrupt?"

The designer shrugged. "Be my guest." Released, she walked past us into the aisle and over to the Salt Box booth.

Nunn waited until she was gone before extending a thin hand to me. It was damp and spotted. I took it. I felt like I was shaking hands with a gecko.

"Ms. Rankin?" Nunn asked, although he clearly knew exactly who I was. "I have heard so much about your Co-op. Excited to meet you." He let his hand slide up my arm as he pulled me aside. The links of a chunky gold bracelet caught on the wool sleeve of my cardigan. "Can I have a moment?" he hummed, guiding me back to the curtains that separated the booth from the rest of the show. "I'd like to set up a time to talk to you about a potential opportunity."

I didn't like Murray Nunn's paw on my arm, and I didn't like Murray. He was so close, his breath told me there had been a decent shot of rum in his morning coffee. I did up the last three buttons of my cardigan. I unclenched myself from his grip.

"Chilly in here, isn't it?" he asked, as any man in a polyester tropical-weight suit in a repurposed hockey rink might. "Give me a minute." Murray reached down and lifted the polyester crepe fabric covering a table.

"Let's warm things up," he smirked.

That was enough.

"Look," I said to the back of his head. "Whatever you want to discuss, Mr. Nunn, I'm not interested. We're already about as economically developed as we need to be on this island. The Crafters and I aren't interested in whatever export-empire building you've got going. We're doing exactly what we want, as much as we want, where we want to do it."

Murray ignored me. Instead, he bent farther down and groped under the draped table like he'd lost a quarter. His narrow pants rode up, and I could see the pale skin of his legs above socks with tiny mallards in diagonal flight across them.

"It's around here somewhere," he fumbled, lifting his head to look at me. "So, you're a negotiator. I like that in a partner."

For some men, words aren't enough. I knew what Murray needed. I reached deep into my ancestral emergency kit and pulled out the famous Rankin women, stop-them-in-their-tracks, *Look*.

It worked.

Maybe too well.

Because one minute Murray Nunn, business talent scout from far away, was leering up at me with his shiny little brown eyes. The next minute, he was flat on his back, those same eyes twice as wide, rolled back in his head, and suddenly as blank as the ducks flying on his socks.

"Murray?" I whispered. What had I done? "Murray?"

The man stretched out on the indoor-outdoor rug on the arena's temporary chipboard floor was as still as the kilted mannequins across the way at Terry's Tartans.

"Murray! What's wrong?" I shouted.

Behind me, I felt the booth fill.

I turned for help. Exhibiters from across the show advanced in a wave. I saw Stuart's nephew Jimmy MacNeil in work boots and canvas overalls, standing between Moira Fraser in her chef apron and Terry in his pom-pommed tam. I saw Darlene, Nancy, and Louise.

Someone screamed.

Phones flashed as they were pulled from pockets. 911 dialed in unison.

"Man's fallen. Knocked out."

"Stroke. Seen it with my uncle."

"Food poisoning. I knew they weren't changing the oil in that fryer."

"In his prime. Younger than I am," a man yelled into his flip phone. "Better get here quick!"

But it was my cousin Darlene who knew what to do.

"Someone go outside and wait for the ambulance," she ordered. "And block the doors to the public entrance. Fast."

Relieved there was a general in charge of the crisis, the volunteers scurried off as deployed. I found a chair and sat down.

"Should we do anything?" I asked Darlene. "Loosen his collar? Mouth to mouth?" I had taken a lifeguard course once in high school. I tried to remember how it was done. I hoped that the lights high in the rink's rafters were responsible for the blue tint on Murray's taut skin.

"The paramedics will be here any minute." Darlene was crisp. "We don't know what's wrong with him, or the best thing to do. Let's wait for the paramedics."

We didn't wait long.

It seemed as if it was only minutes later that the Emergency Health Services crew arrived, two paramedics running with a stretcher down the aisles of knitted socks, handwoven ponchos, homemade jams, live edge turned wooden bowls, and watercolored greeting cards (suitable for framing or sending) as fast as they could, to where Murray lay.

And right behind this convoy was Officer Dawn Nolan of the Royal Canadian Mounted Police, dressed not in her usual dark and epauletted uniform but in a zip-up fleece jacket and jeans. Off duty, but back on the job, Nolan took charge, clipping her RCMP badge to her jacket as she strode toward us.

"Okay, everyone, stand back. Let them work," she commanded, advancing on the crowd like a border collie alone with a flock of sheep. Obediently, we moved back.

Only Darlene, the town's deputy mayor and our natural spokesperson, stayed where she was.

"It's Murray Nunn, a businessman. He was talking to Val here, and then he went down," she explained to Nolan. "I hope he's okay."

Everyone there could see how fast and hard the paramedics were working. A few bystanders muttered it didn't look good and were told to be quiet.

We waited. Then, suddenly, whatever was happening at the back of the booth was over.

The paramedics came out at a trot, and Murray, on the stretcher, a plastic oxygen mask on his face, glided by. Way down the hall, we could see the volunteers hold the big double doors open and the ambulance outside, its engine running.

When the doors closed behind the crew, Nolan turned to us.

"Folks, please complete your setup as promptly as possible. I suggest you secure your booths. If I receive any information on the gentleman's status, I'll let you know."

Nolan looked at me. "Valerie," she said. "I'm going to go set up in the manager's office for the rest of the day, away from the public for a bit. Would you mind coming down and having a chat before you leave? I'd like to go over a few details. Just in case."

I nodded. Darlene and I walked back to our booth. More shaken than we admitted to each other, we arranged and rearranged our display, moving the stand with the macrame plant holders from one side of the booth to the other and then back. We refolded the quilts, restacked the place mats, rehung the stained-glass suncatchers, and rehashed the drama that was Murray Nunn.

"Why did Nolan stay?" I asked my cousin, as I helped her drape old sheets over our table for the night. "What's she doing down in the office? Why does she want to see me? And what's 'just in case' mean? You don't think I did something to Murray, do you? I mean, I gave him *The Look*. You know the one."

"I sure do," Darlene said, "but I doubt if that's what did it. *The Look* only works on husbands as far as I know."

"You're probably right," I agreed. I didn't like the way our tables looked covered. Our crafts looked like ghosts. "I can't put it off any longer. I should see what she wants." Noon had come and gone hours ago, and many of the other exhibitors had left. I was tired, and my mouth was dry. I reached under a table for my bag to pull out my water bottle. Underneath it were the keys for the car I'd left at home.

"I don't believe it. I looked everywhere."

"For what?"

"My keys. Listen, when I'm done with Nolan, do you think you could give me a lift back to the house?"

"Sure, I'll wait. Go on. I want to know what she wants."

Darlene's hand was on my back as I stepped reluctantly out of our booth to make my way down to the rear of the arena. On the other side of the aisle, a flicker of movement at the back of the Re-Creation booth caught my eye. I looked for Louise. She was with Moira Fraser, deep in conversation in front of the Salt Box display.

So, who was in her booth?

A rack of quilted vests rattled aside, and I had my answer.

Stuart's nephew, Jimmy MacNeil, was right near where I had stood with Murray not long ago. For a second, Jimmy was still. Then, after a quick look to the front doors, he parted the curtains behind the table, slipped through, and was gone. But not before I'd had a good look at what he carried under his arm.

Something that someone in a chilly arena might have turned on just before they collapsed.

A portable space heater.

Jimmy thought no one had seen him take it.

But he was wrong.

I had.

CHAPTER FOUR

Dawn Nolan was behind the scarred desk in the rink manager's empty office when I arrived. Her phone was in front of her on a green blotter covered with phone numbers, in a space cleared between the litter of discarded Tim Hortons takeaway cups, and a stapler spread wide and empty, as if someone had meant to fill it but got distracted.

Officer Nolan was not distracted.

"Valerie, would you mind sitting down?" she asked. "I have news."

I picked up a metal-legged chair with a curved plywood seat, like those stacked along the edges of a church hall. I hesitated, then dropped my bag onto the grimy scuffed floor and sat down, spine straight. I felt like a disruptive student called into the principal's office, desperate to make a good impression so no one would call my mother. I pulled my mind away from thinking about Jimmy, Stuart's favorite nephew. A young man who always stopped to pat Toby when we met him on our walks. I remembered how careful and gentle he'd been in the early days when Toby was adjusting to his new home after I'd rescued him. I'd worry about Jimmy later.

I had to pay attention. Why was I here?

"News?" I asked the no-longer-off-duty RCMP officer. "Like what?"

"Murray Nunn," Nolan sighed. "We need to find his next-of-kin before we make a statement, but he died before they made it to the ER today."

I let myself slump in the rickety chair. Someone else's poor mother would be called now. I felt for her. This office was too cold. I shivered and crossed my arms across my chest. There was a small snag on my sleeve.

"He wore a bracelet," I said, "a gold one. Chunky."

"Yes. A medical alert. He had a pacemaker," Nolan said. She picked up the stapler and loaded in the staples, finishing a job someone else had abandoned. "They'll do a report."

"Wow," I said, trying to absorb the news. "Why do you want to talk to me?"

Nolan studied the framed photos of playoff winners on the wall, none of them hanging straight, before she answered me.

"Like I said, just in case. While everything is fresh in your memory." She lifted her phone. "Do you mind if I record this?"

I could hardly say no.

But just in case, what? I wondered again.

"Fill your boots," I said. I wanted to sound matter of fact but realized that my anxiety instead made me sound flippant, and rural.

"Thank you," Nolan said, ignoring my tone. She tapped the surface of her phone. "First. How well did you know Murray Nunn?"

That was an odd question.

"I didn't, not at all. A few people said he was some sort of export organizer guy, maybe interested in doing business with the Co-op. That's it."

"What people told you that?" Nolan asked.

"Louise, the quilted-jacket lady, or should I say designer? Darlene. I can't think of anyone else." I considered adding that Louise hadn't seemed to like Nunn much, and neither had I, but decided against it. He had enough trouble being dead without it being advertised that he was a jerk.

Nolan studied me. "And when you spoke to Mr. Nunn yourself," she continued, "what did you talk about?"

"It was only a few words." This was true, and most of those words had been mine. "I told him we were just fine at the Co-Op, and we weren't interested in doing any exporting."

"Did you now?" Nolan asked, an observation, not a question. "So, you were expecting he wanted a meeting? But you and your group had agreed not to expand?"

I hadn't consulted anyone. I didn't need to.

"No." I said. "I didn't talk to the Crafters. You've got to remember, I had heard nothing about any of this before today. But even if I had talked to them, I knew what they'd think."

Nolan looked down at her phone as if making sure it had heard, and recorded, what I had said. "Interesting. Some of his clients, like Ms. Haggerty, seem to do well. But none of your members would be interested in what he had to offer?"

Nolan waited for me to answer her question. When I didn't, she continued.

"Is there anything else you would like to share about your time with Mr. Nunn? Did he seem unwell to you? Did he say something?"

"No, only that he was a little cold, that's all I remember, but we all were. This is a rink."

"Nothing out of the ordinary? Are you sure?" Nolan persisted.

"Can't think of a thing."

"Anyone else around?"

I tried to visualize the scene in my mind. "Nancy and Louise were at the front of the booth. There was Jeff, the videographer. A few of the other exhibiters in the aisle."

"Hmm," Nolan tapped her phone again and took a moment to think. "Right then, Valerie. That's it for now. But please remember to keep what I told you about Mr. Nunn to yourself. We need to find his family."

"No problem." I wondered what would come next. "Are we going to cancel the show?"

"I don't think so," Nolan said. "As unfortunate as these things are, they can happen at any large event. That booth will be closed, but unless you hear otherwise, the doors for the public will open first thing tomorrow morning."

"Alright, I guess," I said. "But it doesn't feel right."

Nolan got up from behind the desk and walked with me out to the hall.

"No," she said. "It doesn't."

I heard the official announcement of Murray's death on the radio on my way to the show the following day. The announcer said that the cause of death was to be determined, which surprised me. Eager to hear if Darlene had more information, I rushed into our booth, only to find it was the scene of a lecture on Scottish tartans. Terry Kirkpatrick had left his own booth empty to find listeners in ours.

"The unexpected can happen to each of us." Terry removed his tam from his bald head in deference to the man who had left the arena on a stretcher. "That is why knowing who we are in the grand scheme matters. The tartans are living culture. The past giving roots to the present." He turned to the plaid spectacle next door and spread his arms wide in benediction. "And to evolve."

Nancy, a seller of many things, old as well as odd, queried this. "What do you mean, *evolve*?"

Terry took a deep breath. With the doors still locked to the public, it had dawned on him he had a captive audience. It was his dream come true.

"We all know, or we should"—Terry looked at Darlene and me—"that the tartans originated in the Highlands, but they have grown. There is a Sikh tartan and a Jewish tartan officially listed with the Scottish Register of Tartans. After all, everyone has their clan. The Scots understand that. But what matters is genealogical authentication."

"Oh, I know my family history," Nancy said, nudging Darlene in the side. "Tell me, Terry, is there a bootlegger's tartan? That's what my ancestors did. They ran rum down from St. Pierre and Miquelon for Al Capone." There was more than a bit of pride in her voice. During Prohibition, rumrunners from Atlantic Canada had sailed their boats right up to the twelve-mile limit outside New York Harbor. That took guts. "We still have a shed they used down on the old property," she said. "There's metal in the walls. Bulletproof."

"Ingenuity is in our blood," Terry said.

"That's for sure," Nancy agreed, "but remember, bootleggers were ordinary fishermen, only trying to make ends meet outside the system. Being what they had to be." She checked her watch and moved toward her own booth, then stopped to look at us. "Sometimes I think this entire community is like our old shed. So many double lives, so many secrets."

After Nancy left, Terry, Darlene, and I contemplated our own secrets until the videographer walked over to join us.

"Poor old Murray." Jeff shook his head. "We were shooting for an investor's meeting over there"—he pointed to the Salt Box booth—"then this happened." Jeff lowered his heavy camera to the floor, straightened, and then pushed up his sleeves. He wore silver rings on his thumbs and leather thongs wrapped around his wrists. The tattoo on the inside of his forearm read, *Be here now.* He was younger than we were, and it showed. Even so, like most of us, he needed to talk. "I don't believe it."

Darlene reached out and squeezed his arm. "You knew him well. Did you work with Murray often?"

"On and off, you know how it is," Jeff answered. "Whenever Mur signed on a new client, he'd get me to shoot some B-roll for promotions. He'd been at it for years. But lately, business was picking up, so we were doing more together." Jeff leaned in. There was something he needed to share. "Dude was always so tense. I mean, he's my dad's age, at least. It was time he slowed down. I tried to tell him to chill. Do some meditation. But he didn't listen. He always went into the day like he was heading into battle. He was like that yesterday morning at breakfast."

Briefly, I wondered if Murray's stress had anything to do with his collapse. It happened. I'd heard of a man, down the shore, who had dropped dead with his head in a garbage can, mid-search for a missing winning lottery ticket.

"I guess I'll keep going until I figure out what's next." Jeff reached down to pick up his camera. "I suppose this could happen to anyone."

"Maybe not." Nancy was back in our booth, a china teacup in her hand and her face flushed with news. She knocked a stack of baby booties off the table as she moved toward us. "I just got a call from a cousin who works at the hospital. It was his pacemaker," Nancy said breathlessly. "Something went wrong with it. It blew up his heart."

I hoped this was not a literal description. But we all got Nancy's point.

"A problem with his *pacemaker* killed him?" I asked. Nolan must have known this.

"He had a real bad heart, and the pacemaker was supposed to keep it going, but it didn't. And the thing is ... " Nancy looked around to see if anyone else heard her. She had to be careful; her cousin had a good job. "The doctors went into the system and looked at his provincial health records. He had the unit adjusted by his cardiologist in Halifax last week. They can do that, you know, by computer apparently. It was fine then. But when they checked it in the ER, it was off. Real off. A malfunction, but they don't know what caused it. My cousin said the hospital notified the RCMP.

They had to. It's protocol, something about liability, public safety. In case the same thing could happen to someone else who had one." She let this sink in.

Jeff stared at her. I imagined that as a come-from-away, he was startled by the speed, and means, by which this background information had been transmitted. As locals, we weren't. News, particularly bad news, made its way around the community almost before it happened.

"Ah man, poor Murray. Geez, and the RCMP?" Jeff flipped open a small screen near the lens of his camera and spun a few dials. He stared at us. "If they want to know what happened, they better start with me."

"Why is that?" Darlene asked.

"Because." Jeff snapped the viewfinder closed. "I have the whole thing on tape."

CHAPTER FIVE

We stared at him. If we hadn't been in an arena full of noisy craftspeople, we could have heard any of the many pins around us drop.

"You filmed Murray keeling over?" Nancy asked. "You filmed him *dying*?"

"Who knows, maybe." Jeff put his camera down and wiped his hands on his jeans. "I was trying to get a full pan of the Salt Box's front table, the wild herb jellies and the plaque with the family crest, before the crowds came. I had to move over here to do it. But the angle meant that, at the edge of the frame, I caught a good view of the back of the next booth. I saw you, Valerie, and Murray. When I zoomed in, I caught your argument."

"Argument?" Darlene gave me her version of the Rankin women *Look*. I was not only her cousin; I was also her best friend. She was supposed to be first to know about any heated discussions I had.

I had no clue what Jeff was talking about. Then, I remembered. My speech of resistance. The words I used when I had told Murray the Co-Op had no interest in business expansion or markets that weren't local. I knew I had a voice that carried. It had gotten me into trouble in school. I suspected Jeff had captured not only the scene at the back of the Re-Creation booth but also the angry tone of my voice.

"Hmm," Nancy said. "I wonder if that was why Murray got so upset that ... "

I tried to stop Nancy before she got to the blown-out-heart part. I didn't want to hear that again. No one did.

"All I did was tell the man we weren't interested in his consulting services," I tried to explain. I waved my arm in a be-my-guest gesture to the end of the aisle. "There's a Mountie still set up down in the manager's office. If you've got something in there"—I pointed at Jeff's bulky camera—"she might want to see it."

"The right thing to do," Darlene prompted.

"Yeah," Jeff said. "Yeah. I'll show her. See you ladies later," he added. "Or not."

Nancy, Darlene, and I watched him head down to see Nolan.

"How awful," my cousin whispered to me when he was gone. "But don't worry. I'm sure none of this is your fault." She paused. "Or at least not most of it."

Surprisingly, considering the drama that preceded it, the afternoon and next day of the show were, from a retail point of view, a success. Our booth attracted the largest crowd. The news of Murray's collapse brought curious shoppers in to linger, *right across from where that man dropped dead*, and to make purchases to disguise why they were there. Louise Haggerty, her own booth off-limits, moved many of her jackets and vests to other booths for sale, on the condition that customers were told they'd come from the scene of the tragedy.

This was poor taste, but good for her sales.

But by the end of day two, when a cowbell rang to announce the end of the event, Darlene and I were down to our last nerves.

"Enough is enough," my cousin said. "All I want to do is go home, lie on the couch with my cats, and let George feed me dinner. Do you want to come over?"

George Kosoulas's food tempted me. Darlene's new husband, whom we had both known since high school, had learned to cook at his parents' Greek restaurant, the only restaurant in Gasper's Cove.

"That sounds wonderful," I told her. "Particularly the lying on the couch with the cats part, but Stuart and I are having an official date night." I glanced over at Nancy, her head deep in a box of unsold figurines. She hadn't heard me.

"Date night?" Darlene smirked. "This is a recent development, isn't it?"

I dodged.

"A client gave Stuart a gift certificate to the Salt Box," I said vaguely, looking across to Moira's booth. It was already nearly empty, efficiently cleaned out by staff from the restaurant. Only the draped tables, stained here and there with dribbles of sticky toffee and melted sea buckthorn sorbet, remained. "We couldn't waste it."

Darlene rolled her eyes. "Whatever you say. But don't make my mistake, Val. Don't let time pass you by."

This wasn't the first time I'd heard this. "I won't. You're as bad as Nancy."

"You think? Maybe we both just want the best for you. Is Stuart coming here to get you? Or do you need a ride home?"

"A ride would be good. If you can drop me off, I'll have time to walk Toby. I'm meeting Stuart at the restaurant. He had to go back to the yacht club. Some kind of trouble with the Sail By."

"Trouble?" Darlene snapped the lid on the last of our big plastic storage bins. The store's handyman, Duck MacDonald, would pick them up later. "You're kidding. What kind?"

"No idea," I said. "Stuart is all worked up about it. But the Sail By is only a spring boat parade. What could go wrong with that?"

As it turned out, plenty could go wrong, and it had.

Stuart and I were at a table near the back of the restaurant, waiting for a mysterious first course of "haggis bonbons," when he pulled a fountain pen and an envelope from the inside pocket of his tweed sports jacket to sketch out the problem. Stuart was the only person I knew who used a fountain pen, or owned one. But in his hand, even with his index finger marked with blue, it looked like it belonged. The pen reflected Stuart's belief that what worked should be left as it was. Sometimes, I wondered if he felt that way about us.

Tonight, he used his pen to draw. As I watched him work, I saw the blue-lined outline of the ragged coastline of the north shore of Gasper's Island take shape. To this, Stuart added dots to mark the locations of the yacht club, the look-off, and the Bluenose Inn, owned by another one of my cousins, Rollie Rankin. What I did not understand were the edges along the coast, which he shaded in with careful engineer cross-hatching.

"What are those?" I asked, leaning back to let the server put a small plate in front of each of us. The haggis bonbons, nested in spruce twigs, surrounded by swirled sauce, looked a lot like the frozen meatballs I had at home in the fridge. "The places you're shading?"

"Our problems," Stuart said. "We follow the same route every year with the boats. It's one that gives the islanders a good view of the parade. The sailors kill themselves decking out those boats. You know that."

"Tell me about it," I said. Many Crafters, related to various boat owners, helped them decorate.

"Yes, you'd know." Stuart said, putting the cap back on his pen. "So much work. So much effort. That's why we try to keep close to shore, so everyone can see us pass. It's tradition."

I understood. The club's annual boat parade marked the beginning of the recreational sailing season. No one in the community missed the Sail By, a floating parade of decorated vessels. The boats themselves were varied and democratically represented. Some were modest thirty-footers, like Stuart's own, some retired working lobster boats, and some larger yachts, with Nova Scotia flags at the bow and the American flags of the home ports at the stern. The judges gave the best-decorated boat a prize—a battered old cup, which they immediately returned to a glass case in the boathouse. But the Sail By wasn't about the competition. It was about the community, the party, and, most of all, the end of the long winters when we were trapped inside by the cold.

I ate one of the bonbons, washed it down with my wine, and then picked up Stuart's map. I noticed, on closer inspection, that his inked areas formed an almost alternating pattern along the coast, like a knitting chart.

"What am I looking at?" I asked. The marked sections ran in a broken line from the yacht club to the old fish plant. My memory of that coast only saw decaying cliffs, dry sea grass, and rocks.

"There's nothing there," I said. "No decent beaches. Only rocks and water. That's why no one has built anything. No roads, only walking paths to places along the shore to watch the boats. Nothing else there. Why are these parts of land important? I don't understand."

"Bingo." Stuart popped a haggis bonbon into his mouth. "You nailed it. First try."

"I did?" The server took away our empty plates and even the cutlery we hadn't used. This was a classy place. "Is this about access to watch the boats? About who owns that land?"

"You're hot tonight." Stuart beamed at me. Part of me wished he was referring to my new dress, hemmed only the night before, but I knew he was still talking about rocky land. "Random edges of municipal land, pieces of rocky beach or cliffs," he continued, "totally unsuitable for any kind of development or road work. However, someone divided and bought it. It's making me crazy trying to figure out why. I mean, these are useless properties, some of them small, less than a quarter of an acre, so who would want them? I thought the municipality planned to use these undeveloped parcels, this useless land, for nesting plovers. Until they were sold to private, undisclosed owners over the winter." He paused while heavy stoneware plates, stacked with lamb on mashed potatoes, were carefully placed in front of us.

I took a careful stab in the dim light at the potato tower, not wanting to topple another craftsperson's work. The Salt Box was a few steps down from street level in what had been, in other days, a merchant's basement. Old boards had been removed during the renovations to expose the rough-hewn, dungeon-like granite blocks of the original masonry. The only windows, dark at night, were small slits near the ceiling. The space was illuminated by lighting hidden behind eaves at the top of the walls, so it slanted out in dusky beams, and by tall flickering lamps on each table, evoking intimacy, romance, and the past. The rough linen of the napkins reinforced the atmosphere, as did the framed remnants of ancient Fraser tartan and old family records mounted near each table. Moira cared, and it showed. But behind the thoughtful decor, I sensed something musty and claustrophobic.

I ate and waited for Stuart to tell me more. Finally, he put his fork down. I sensed he was working up to asking me for a favor. I had no idea what it would be, but I knew, before he asked, I would do it.

"First thing you want to know is who is buying up this property and why. Am I right?" I asked.

"You got it. As an engineer who does work for the town, I got into the property records, but all those show is the name of a holding company. Saltire Investments."

"Saltire? As in St. Andrew's Cross?" I asked. "The one on the flag of Scotland and our flag here in Nova Scotia?"

"Yes, exactly," Stuart said. "That's the only saltire I know."

"The name must mean something," I said. "Maybe tell you who this company is?"

"You'd think so," Stuart said. "But I can't seem to track down who they are. The records are blind. That's where I'm hoping you can help me."

"Me? How?"

"Your sewing classes at the store."

This was a leap. As far as I knew, none of the students in *Knits for the Terrified* were real-estate tycoons.

"Explain that one."

Stuart refolded his napkin. "Fair enough. Look, I tried to feel the mayor out about this, but he clammed up. That means he is involved. It's got to be about money. You know the municipality's strapped for cash."

I did. Darlene had told me about the budget shortfall created by the mayor's pet projects, such as the parking meters (twenty-five cents an hour) he had installed on streets no one parked on. Some of the younger Crafters had yarn-bombed them for laughs.

"I know money's tight, but what does that have to do with my sewing classes?"

Stuart leaned forward and took my hand. Off in the corner, I saw the server smile. She probably assumed we were a sweet, middle-aged couple having a romantic dinner, not two people discussing the sale of useless land.

"I think the mayor has been meeting with the purchasers," Stuart said. "I can't find out who. The only person who might know is his executive assistant. She's new to town. I don't really know her well. But"—I could tell Stuart had done some detecting—"when I was last in the municipal offices, I asked her how she was settling in. She said great, she'd made friends through some classes she was taking." He leaned back, pleased with himself. "At Rankin's General Store. Run by that marvelous sewing teacher, Valerie Rankin."

I let the compliment pass and took a sip of water before I allowed myself to react.

"Okay. What I'm hearing is you want me to drill the mayor's EA on his appointment calendar while I teach sewing? Sometime between the rib necklines and twin-needle hemming?"

Stuart nodded.

"How am I supposed to do that?" I asked. "In a nonobvious way?"

Stuart squeezed my hand and released it. The server advanced tentatively with the dessert menu.

"You'll think of something," Stuart said. "You're creative. But something's fishy, and I need you to go fishing."

CHAPTER SIX

As I got ready for my class the next evening, I felt the not-unfamiliar conflicting emotions of guilt and anticipation. On the one hand, the side that my mother would have been proud of, I was ashamed I had agreed to use my position of sewing-room authority to trick the mayor's innocent and young new executive assistant into giving me none-of-my-business information. On the other hand, I felt energized to be working on solving a mystery of any kind, but particularly one that involved Stuart Campbell.

This was unfamiliar territory for us. I had known Stuart, the quirky father of one of my younger crafters, for a while. He'd helped me convert the unused second floor of the family store into a place for local crafters to sell on consignment. Then, we'd become dog-walking partners, me with Toby, he with his little Nova Scotia Duck Toller, Birdie. With the unhurried speed of a porcupine crossing a rural road, we were on the verge of romance. I sometimes wondered if the delay was my fault. It seemed to me that Stuart always helped me out and that I was the one who always needed helping. Part of me was waiting for my turn to even things up before the next stage. Whatever that was.

Maybe this would be that opportunity.

However, when my students arrived, it was Nancy Mullins, enrolled to learn how to insert bust darts in a pattern that didn't have them, who beat me to the punch.

After a quick scan of the room from the doorway, Nancy spotted Heidi Wallace, the mayor's executive assistant, diligently winding her bobbin. Without pause, Nancy bustled over to deposit her vintage Singer Featherweight next to the young woman.

"Drive here yourself?" Nancy asked Heidi while pretending to look under the table for the power outlet. "Or did you get a ride? With someone?"

Heidi cut a thread and picked up her bobbin case before answering. She was a careful seamstress, meticulously constructing a knit dress. She was new to sewing and worried about making mistakes. I knew she'd be a good garment maker if she relaxed. Getting her there, besides picking her brain in a dishonest way, was my main assignment as her teacher.

As she jiggled her bobbin into place, Heidi looked up at Nancy. "I came here myself. It doesn't take long to get here from work in Drummond. Across the causeway is practically door-to-door."

"Right. You work for the mayor, don't you?" I asked, inserting myself into the conversation, as if I didn't know where Heidi worked. Stuart would be proud of me.

Nancy sat down and moved her chair close to Heidi.

"Municipal offices? Not many young people over there, are there? It must be hard for someone your age, new to the town, to make friends." Nancy did her best to imitate an innocent, well-meaning older aunt. "Or do you go back to Halifax on the weekends? To see a boyfriend, maybe?"

Heidi sighed softly, but I caught it. This was not the first time she'd been asked a question like this. "No boyfriend," she said. "My work keeps me busy."

My turn.

"I can imagine," I said. "You do all the mayor's arrangements. You must deal with a lot of different people during the run of a day."

Nancy had let me volley but now moved in closer to the net.

"You must work so hard. Apart from sewing with us, what else do you do in your spare time? Bowl, perhaps?" she asked.

Heidi paused in threading the needle on her machine. "No. Not since birthdays when I was a kid."

"Go to the gym?"

Heidi shook her head.

"Nightlife? Out to the bars with friends?" Nancy appeared to be working down some list in her mental matchmaker Rolodex.

"Not much of a drinker," Heidi said. She put the presser foot down and stepped on the foot control, a serious worker concentrating on her dress.

"Bird-watching?" Nancy was getting desperate. She searched the room for inspiration.

Just then, our handyman, Duck MacDonald, walked past the open door of the classroom. Duck was single, his dating life interrupted by a stint in Drummond Correctional Institute.

"What are your views on the criminal justice system?" Nancy asked. "And those wrongfully convicted?"

I'd heard enough. I grabbed the ball. Poor Heidi needed rescuing. And I still needed information.

"Back to your job," I said to Heidi. I didn't have much time. The rest of my students were trickling in. I'd have to earn my sewing teacher's fee soon. "The people who the mayor sees are locals, are they? Or people from away?"

"A mix," Heidi answered. She seemed to appreciate the conversational diversion. "A few are summer residents or real-estate people applying for zoning variances, things like that. Some just want to know about deals they can cut with the council for development; others are looking for funding, contacts, or contracts. Like that designer, Miss Haggerty, who is in town."

Heidi stopped herself to study me. This girl was often underestimated. I knew the type; I knew the look. My curiosity was under assessment.

"But really, most of our meetings are regular business," she hurried on. We were getting close to the last word she wanted to say on this subject. "Tradespeople with contracts with the town. Ray's Haul-em for cleanups. Sparky's for special electrical work. Snow-clearing companies in the winter. Photo shoots for the paper for events."

Nancy jumped back into the game.

"Events? Like the craft show this past weekend? The one that opened late because of that poor man who died?" She turned to the other students, who were listening. "We were there, you know. Me and Valerie, at our booths. We saw it all."

"Yes, we were close," I admitted.

"Yes, that's right. Busy show." Nancy moved on to refocus on Heidi. "They brought in a nice young man to wire the place up. Very polite. He will do well for himself. Electricians make good money, you know, more than you might think. What's his name again, Val? Stuart's nephew?" Nancy knew who Jimmy was but wanted it said out loud.

"Jimmy," I complied.

I'd lost this round, but I had played against a master. I turned to the rest of the students.

"Ladies, let's sew."

After class, Stuart met me at the edge of the schoolyard for our evening dog walk. The store was near the causeway that separated the mainland from our island and Gasper's Cove. Toby and I lived in a bungalow on the hill up the road from the store. The high school and junior high, joined by a common sports field, was at the end of my street and perfect for off-leash dog walking. Doing this together with our two dogs was getting to be a regular thing for us, begun because Stuart said his new dog needed company, and continued because we, the humans, did too. Now, after the long dark winter, the spring evenings were light enough for the four of us to do a full circuit around the school track. There, we sometimes saw Officer Wade Corkum, the head of the local RCMP detachment, pounding his way around the oval. Other times, the only occupants of the field were teenage couples on the playground swings, getting to know each other.

This evening, Stuart led the way to a far corner of the field so we could talk in private.

"How was your class?" he asked.

"Good. Fun. The course is about fear. It's so much easier to sew a knit than a woven fabric, but many sewers don't believe that. I spend the four weeks getting them to trust themselves."

"Interesting," Stuart said politely, until he could ask me about Heidi. "And after these four weeks, what do they have?"

"A T-shirt. Front, back, sleeves. Crew neckline. The V necklines we do in the *Knits for the No Longer Terrified* class. I'm doing that one in the fall."

"Okay." Stuart had two balls in his pocket, and he threw them, one for each dog. Toby and Birdie shot off down the field like rockets propelled by joy. "Did you have time to feel out that student of yours, the mayor's EA? About any visitors? Ones who might be interested in coastal property?"

"Heidi? I tried, but I wasn't the only one with an agenda. Nancy Mullins was there, trying to set her up with your nephew."

Stuart laughed. "I can imagine. Nancy's been stalking Jimmy for weeks. I had to hide him from her in the international aisle at the Foodmart last time we were there."

"Down there with the Vegemite and coconut milk?" I laughed. "I don't blame him. She can be relentless, and he's definitely on her to-do list."

Toby was back. He dropped a saliva-covered ball at my feet and backed up, waiting for the next throw. Stuart reached down and heaved the fluorescent tennis ball past the goalposts on the football field.

"Now, about Heidi." I tried to remember. "I couldn't find out much. The mayor's meetings seem pretty routine.

Zoning stuff from summer residents, local contractors, and a few people trying to do business." But one name had caught my attention. "One of those was Louise Haggerty. Does that count?"

"That woman with the lumpy jackets?" Stuart asked. "I don't think so." Off in the distance, Wade had stopped his circuits around the track. He waved and started to walk over. "The zoning issues may be where this is at," Stuart said, waving back to Wade. "My next step might be the planning office to have a closer look at the property records and zoning applications. There may be something there that gives me a hint at who Saltire is."

"Sorry I wasn't able to solve any mysteries," I said. "I was under a lot of pressure—rib versus bound necklines, optional bust darts, a marriage broker in the class." I tried to think of other angles. "But give me time. I know everybody, and for sure someone knows what's going on."

"Worth a try," Stuart said. "I know this seems silly, but I love the Sail By. It's something we do, like every other small yacht club in the province. Folks stand on shore and are happy. It's like the whole community is launching us into the summer. It's fun, and it matters. If we can't do it the way we've always done it, all around the island, I want to know why."

Wade had passed the spectator stands at the end of the playing field. He pulled the towel around his neck and caught up with Toby. He ruffled the dog's blond head as he walked over.

Wade nodded to me and turned to Stuart. "Stu," he said, "how's it going?"

"Can't complain. You?"

"Keeping busy."

Inside, I rolled my eyes. Male dogs were the same, I knew, looking at Birdie and Toby. Lots of circling and marking territory before anything else happened, before any real talk could start.

"Same old, same old, eh?" Stuart volunteered.

I stepped in.

"I saw Officer Nolan over the weekend," I said to Wade. "When that man who passed away was taken out of the show. We were lucky she was there. She handled it well." I caught myself, aware of what I was doing. Wade was the senior officer in the detachment and Dawn Nolan's boss. There were those in Gasper's Cove, mainly me and Darlene, who thought that Wade's seniority was based more on his reputation as a former almost-National Hockey League star than on his superior law-enforcement skills. Nolan, we suspected, was the more formidable investigator. If I had been leading a life of crime, it would be her, and not her boss, who would worry me most.

"Yes. I read the report," Wade said. "The next morning." He turned to Stuart. "I was off when it happened. Fly-fishing for salmon in Cape Breton."

"Lucky you," Stuart said. "How did those new lures work out?"

"Like a charm. Trying something new." Wade drew back his arm and let go as if he was casting a line.

"Really? Bring them along to bowling on Thursday. I'd like to have a look," Stuart said.

I had to interrupt again.

"I've heard from a few people," I said, clipping Toby's leash to his collar, "that Mr. Nunn died of a heart attack. Something to do with his pacemaker? Terrible thing."

For a second, a cloud of confusion crossed over Wade's face until he caught it and tucked it away. "Heart attack? Not sure that they would describe it as that. The statement from the hospital is that he had a long-standing condition, but that something may have interfered with his pacemaker to set off his cardiac arrest." He narrowed his eyes at me. "Who told you about this?"

"Not sure, around." This was no time to involve Nancy and, indirectly, her unprofessional relative. I countered with a question of my own. "What do you mean, 'interfered' with it?" I tried to remember what I had told Nolan at the arena. That I had seen nothing unusual and, therefore, had nothing to report. But then, I remembered Jeff. "There was a film, someone shooting it for the restaurant."

"Got it. Seen it," Wade said.

As he was listening, I could see Stuart's engineering brain go into gear, considering possibilities. "A pacemaker?" he asked. "A lot of things can interfere with the current, the signal, and throw it off. A cell phone, smartwatch, radios, an airport scanner, an appliance ... "

"Like those signs they have up in restaurants?" I asked. "About not going near the microwave with a pacemaker?" Moira had given out samples of hot hors d'oeuvres. How had she heated them up?

"Those are all possibilities," Wade conceded. "I've got Officer Nolan checking it out now."

"Maybe Val's onto something," Stuart said. "Was there a microwave nearby?" He had read my mind.

"There was," Wade said. "And Nolan said the booth had one of those tall things, like an upright vacuum with a tank of water ... "

"A clothes steamer," I corrected. "After Louise unpacked, she needed to get the wrinkles out before the garments were on display."

"That's a possibility," Stuart nodded. "And everyone these days has a cell phone or smartwatch. From what I understand, all it would take would be someone getting close to a pacemaker with it. Geez, a hug could even do it, I guess, if a person's heart was that vulnerable. An accident."

This idea caught Wade's attention. I could see he was filing it away for later retrieval as something he'd thought of himself. "Good thinking, Stu. That might be what did it. Fits with what I figure. An innocent action with unforeseen consequences. Something ordinary that went wrong." He shook his head. "Nolan wants to eliminate foul play. I don't see any evidence of that myself, but it's not going to hurt for her to check it out. But I agree with you, Stu, not a bad idea, that cell phone thing. I'll pass it on to her." He leaned toward Stuart, glancing sideways at me. "She's a great officer but doesn't have all my experience. She'll get there. There's no substitute for experience."

Or maybe there was.

Nolan operated on instinct.

So did I.

And in the weak evening light, I felt a breeze coming up the hill from the ocean, carrying a small quiet voice. It told me I had to talk to Stuart about his nephew. After we left Wade and were leading the dogs out of the field, I tried.

"Wade runs; so does Jimmy, doesn't he? We pass him in the mornings. How's he doing these days?"

"Okay, I think," Stuart answered. "I'd like to see him find something with a future. He's a smart kid; he could do better. Run his own company, even."

"Have you told him that?"

"I tried to, but I need to be careful. His dad was an electrician, and so was his grandfather. He'd applied to Dalhousie University to do engineering, but when his father died, he switched to the community college to follow their trade. Grief, I suppose. I respect that, but ... " Stuart struggled to find the right words. "I've always had a soft spot for him. He's a quiet guy, much like myself. I don't like the idea that he isn't appreciated, you know?"

Yes, I did. I also knew this was no time for me to tell Stuart what I had seen Jimmy remove from the show. This was delicate territory, family territory.

Something was not right, but what that was, I would have to find out on my own.

I was back at work in the store the next day when the opportunity to set my mind at rest presented itself. Colleen, my aunt and Darlene's mom, and I were going over the accounts when the bell over the front door rang.

Colleen poked me in the ribs. "Look who the wind blew in. Sparky Bailey, the guy I've been trying to chase down for days."

I looked up from the accounts-receivable spreadsheet. The head of the electrical firm named after himself sidled into our store with his best worker, Jimmy MacNeil, a step behind him. Sparky usually bought his supplies in Drummond, but lately, with work on the island, he'd dropped by to pick up odds and ends from us: wire, connectors, a bit here and there. But after a month, it had added up. And so far, Sparky hadn't paid for any of it.

As manager, collecting was my responsibility. I nodded to Colleen and made my way around the counter to greet them.

Sparky and Jimmy were quite a pair. Jimmy was in his late twenties, and Sparky at least twenty-five years older. Jimmy, who had inherited the Campbell curly hair and disconcertingly blue eyes from his mother, was dressed like a model from Mark's Work Wearhouse—clean steel-toed boots, tan canvas overalls, yellow leather gloves in the back pocket, and a gray long-sleeved henley. When he saw me, Jimmy took off his blue hard hat and smiled.

Sparky left his hat on. Ignoring me, he hurried in the direction of the electrical aisle in the rear of the store.

I intercepted him.

"Sparky, just the man I want to see," I said, positioning myself between the electrical contractor and a bucket of spring leaf rakes. I wrapped my hand around one of them, in case I would need it to block access to the aisle.

"In a hurry, my girl," Sparky said. The untied laces of his work boots slapped on the worn boards of the floor as he barreled forward. "Got other people's screw-ups to fix up today. These clients are running me off my feet. Got to get it all done by next Friday." He looked over at Jimmy, who was examining the pressed-metal ceiling overhead. "Got to work with the staff I have. Heaven help me." A wisp of affection, or maybe of nostalgia, drifted across Sparky's face and then was banished. "I was like this young fellow here when I started, I admit that. Which is why I have to show him the ropes. That's how I learned, tough love. You've got a business. You know what I'm talking about."

"Yes, I do. Business. As in, past-thirty-days business," I added, as if I were discussing the weather. "Time to settle up your account, *my boy*."

Sparky stopped and plastered a bewildered expression on his face, as if he had no idea what I was talking about. He hitched up a pair of old gray sweatpants that looked like he had worn them every day for the past ten. The maneuver gave Colleen and me an unsolicited view of a hairy belly and a navel under the layers of a stained navy T-shirt and open plaid shirt.

Colleen turned away.

"Jimmy, didn't you take care of that?" Sparky threw the question at his assistant. "I can't be everywhere doing everything myself. I thought you were on top of things."

Jimmy answered with a patience that came from practice. "I did what you told me, boss; I told them to put it on our account. If I was supposed to do something different, I would have."

Sparky snorted, reached into his back pocket, and pulled out a roll of bills held together with an elastic band. It occurred to me that Sparky Bailey did a fair amount of cash-only, under-the-table work. He sighed with what was meant to sound like his last breath, or the very end of his patience, and peeled off a few hundred-dollar bills as if they were his own skin.

"Here you go, Val, that should do it. Wire, about 30 meters of it." He shook his pumpkin head under the hard hat perched on top like an ill-fitting salad bowl. "The apprentice here didn't get the truck loaded up right to come over. We got no time to go back over the causeway for supplies."

I took the bills and handed them to Colleen. "Thanks," I said. "I'll cut the wire for you."

Now that I had Sparky's money, I was happy for him to leave. Until then, I chatted.

"Where's the job here?" I asked. "Don't you do most of your work over in Drummond?"

"Usually," Sparky conceded, striding down the main aisle beside me, Jimmy behind us. Out of the corner of my eye, I saw Shadow, the store cat, crouched low under the last shelf in the plumbing aisle, her eyes on the waving laces of Sparky's boots, ready to pounce. "But the pressure's on. When you are the only outfit in town with a reputation like ours, it's hard to keep up. I've got a job to wrap up for one of those summer people with a big house on Shore Road, then I got to get over to the fish plant and hook up some new equipment, and after that, there's that place that needs rewiring."

"Sounds like a lot," I sympathized. I wasn't sure, but a flicker in Jimmy's eye looked like a wink. "The fish plant?" The fish-processing plant on the north side of the island had been in operation since the 1950s but hadn't been active as such for a few years. "I didn't think there were enough fish for it to reopen."

"There isn't," Sparky said with an authority he enjoyed. "Most of the fish these days are processed out at sea. Caught and packed. Those jokers out there at the old plant make the plastic containers for shipping live lobsters." He leaned in closer. "Got to be some government money in it to make it out here on the island. The way of the world, I guess." He paused, making sure I was listening before he explained to me how the world worked. "A lesson there, my girl. No future in thinking small, just because that's how it's always been done. These days, if you want to stay in business, you got to think global. Take that sewing operation. Our rewiring job. Industrials and pressing machines can't run that on old wiring, which is good for me." He motioned me closer. "Change of subject," he whispered. "Colleen's holding up pretty well these days, isn't she? Always took care of herself, that woman. I might want to catch up."

Sparky hoisted up his oil-stained sweatpants again and retied the drawstring under his belly. "You get the wire there," he instructed Jimmy. "Try not to screw it up. I'll be out front when you're finished."

Jimmy and I were silent as we watched Sparky amble away to harass Colleen, unaware that Shadow was right behind him, stalking the tantalizing, untied shoelaces of the contractor's boots.

"My money's on the cat," Jimmy said.

I laughed. Jimmy helped me lift the giant spool of wire, and we counted off the 30 meters together.

"What does he mean, 'sewing machines'?" I asked as we wrapped up the wire. How was it possible that anyone in the community needed industrial machines and pressers and I didn't know about it?

"Oh, that," Jimmy said. "It's something Terry the kilt guy is setting up. He's bringing in clan tartan from Scotland and making kilts to order locally, to avoid the import duties.

Terry figures once he gets it going, he'll make a killing with weddings and things like that. He's got an old family cottage he wants to set up. Not sure he has a clue what he's doing." Jimmy hesitated. He usually didn't say this much, so I gave him time. "It was that guy who died at the craft show who talked him into it. He got Terry some deal on industrial equipment from down the South Shore. Trouble is that the steam pressers need more voltage. You know what that means."

I did. Rankin's electrical aisle was one of our busiest. "The wiring in an old cottage wouldn't be up to it."

"Exactly," Jimmy said. "Same as a house. We use 110–120 in our houses, except for the dryers and ovens. They need 240, like anything that heats up, same as these presses, I guess. When we upgrade the wiring at Terry's place, we're going to add in a couple of 240-volt outlets and a 30-amp circuit breaker."

"Funny, when I saw Terry at the show, he didn't mention any of this to me," I said. I was put out with the tartan retailer. Was there some reason he had kept his plans to himself?

"Who has Terry got lined up to do his sewing?" I asked. I tried to keep my voice small, talk light. "Anyone I know?" I tried to think of who I had seen chatting with Terry in his booth over the weekend. "Someone who was at the show, maybe?"

"The show?" Jimmy asked. "I wouldn't know. I was there early in the morning to wire it up. But I left before it started."

I stopped walking and stared at Stuart's nephew.

That, I knew, was a lie.

CHAPTER SEVEN

After Colleen added the charge for the wire to Sparky's account, the two men left. Sparky was the first to go, indignant that he had failed to charm Colleen. Jimmy followed, pausing briefly to rub his hand over Toby's soft golden retriever head, as if it were a good-luck charm, or maybe only for comfort.

The big dog was used to this. He came to work with me at the store most days and spent them in an old recliner near the door to Front Street, close to the window and the activity of the wharf across the street. Older customers who missed dogs they had lost long ago lingered beside that chair. Small children slipped him the soggy remnants of sugar-free cookies when they thought no one was looking. Summer visitors called him our Walmart greeter. Locals called him a very good boy.

So, now after the bell had chimed once, and the door had closed behind the two electricians, one noisy and one quiet, Toby jumped into his station and curled up. He had a plan for the day. I didn't. I needed a second opinion, advice, or some wisdom.

"Colleen, can I ask you a question?"

"What about?" My aunt closed the cash drawer and turned to me.

"Who this is about doesn't matter," I began, "but what would you do if you saw someone do something strange, but you weren't sure how to ask them about it, because if you did, there was a chance you would cause bad feelings with someone else?"

Colleen tightened her cardigan around her and thought. With a large family, none of them ordinary, she had extensive experience with tricky conversations.

"My first question to you would be, why does it matter? We all do strange things from time to time. I spent twenty minutes yesterday trying to find my glasses. They were on top of my head."

"It matters because something serious happened, and this person might have had something to do with it." There. I'd said it. Something I hadn't entirely admitted to myself.

A canny look crossed Colleen's face. "Like someone shoplifting?" she asked.

This was an obvious question. Harry Sutherland had once peeled off a $1.99 sticker from a package of seeds and tried to reapply it to a $30 shovel.

"No, nothing to do with the store," I said. "Somewhere else." Being evasive was exhausting. I usually told my aunt everything, and we both knew that.

Colleen pulled out the stool from behind the counter and sat down. This was a signal she was ready to give her advice.

"Valerie, I know you like to ... what do we want to call it? Get all involved in things. Sometimes it's been helpful to people, and even the RCMP, and sometimes it's not." Colleen twisted her rings on her fingers while she thought. Darlene did her mother's nails. The latest edition was bright turquoise with tiny stars on the index fingers. I knew my aunt was working hard not to hurt my feelings. "You might want to think about not getting carried away. It's not a good thing to get into the habit of seeing trouble in innocent situations." I could tell Colleen was desperate to ask who we were talking about but holding herself back.

"But my intuition," I argued. "Something doesn't feel right."

"Well, then. In that case." The Rankin touch of the fey was not to be disregarded. "Before you say or do anything that might hurt someone, I would watch this person and see if they do anything else."

"Good idea." Her warning made sense. I would find a way to keep an eye on Jimmy. Subtly. Tomorrow. Or even again today.

Colleen seemed to read my mind.

"You be careful, my dear," she said. "It's never a good idea to write off to malice what can be explained by accident or incompetence."

As I walked back to my office, I tried to think of unobtrusive ways I could watch Jimmy MacNeil. It would not be easy. A middle-aged sewing teacher and general store manager couldn't just show up at an electrician's workplace and go unnoticed. I had to be creative. And that, as it usually was, was my answer.

I would create my own job site and deputize my own watcher.

Duck MacDonald was stacking heavy bags of lime and grass seed for spring lawns near the landing inside the store's back door when I found him.

"Working late," I said.

"Yeah, well, some of the boys are home. I'm staying clear until they move on."

The boys, I knew, were other members of the MacDonald clan, the always-in-trouble-with-the-law branch of Duck's large family.

"I thought most of them were still in jail," I said.

"Not the old fellows," he sighed. "They have a routine. Lift something every fall, just enough for a warm bed and three meals a day in the winter, and then out in the spring. Some folks go to Florida in the winter. My family goes into the slammer." Duck tried to laugh; he'd told this story before. "And some of the other guys go in for a misdemeanor when they need to lie low for a while. The prison's like a second home for them. One of my cousins even calls it his head office, like he's some genius tricking the government into covering his overhead. Jail can be a safe place for some characters, I guess." Duck grunted. "Unless they're a snitch. Those guys don't last too long. Revenge is as important to a crook as money."

Shadow appeared from behind the bags of seed. She rubbed herself against Duck's legs to show her support, sympathy, and reassurance. Like me, she knew how hard it was for Duck to talk about his own time in prison. After all, the only reason he had done time was because he'd been set up by the incompetence of his own brothers. Who else but one of the MacDonalds would have printed currency all with the same serial numbers? Who else would have sent him into a shop to spend it?

For Duck's sake, I wanted to change the subject. My cousin Rollie had met Duck while working as a psychologist at the local penitentiary. When Duck was released, Rollie had hired him on as handyman at our store. Always a good worker, Duck usually didn't talk this much, except to Shadow, who was easing him in.

The cat looked up at me. *Talk about something else*, she coached.

"Are we still blowing that fuse in the basement?" I asked. I knew we were.

"Why?" Duck looked uneasy. Although an honest man himself, he had inherited the family tendency to look guilty when questions were asked. "I've been careful not to run too many things off the one circuit. But"—he looked to the front of the store and to Colleen and then away—"hard for everyone to remember to do that, though."

"You're right," I agreed. I paid little attention to this myself. "But we need someone to look at it." I paused, careful not to offend Duck by suggesting we bring in outside help. "How about Stuart's nephew? Young guy, maybe could use a little extra?"

Duck lifted another bag of lawn seed and placed it on the pile. "You mean Jimmy MacNeil? Who was just in here? I already know him from Thursday nights. Meetings at the church. I can ask him. I put in some wire myself, but unless it's done by a licensed electrician, it wouldn't pass inspection."

It was news to me that Duck attended any church-type meetings. I waited for more information, and when he offered none, I continued with my own agenda.

"Thanks, I'd appreciate that." This part was easy; the rest of it might not be. "Such a nice guy, but he seems to have something on his mind." And under his arm, too, but I didn't say that. "Anything going on with him?" This sounded weak, but it was all I could think of.

Duck stopped adjusting the corners of the stacked seed bags so they were even and stood up. He brushed his hands on his pant legs. "He's good. Kinda strange thing to ask me, if you don't mind me saying."

He was right.

"Oh, I know, it's just ... " I could hear myself scramble. "His uncle and I are sort of dating." There was a pleading tone in my voice that embarrassed me but was necessary. "I'm trying to get to know the family better. It might help me get in good with Stuart." I stopped talking as I waited for the bolt of lightning reserved for poor liars to come down and strike me.

Instead, Duck relaxed.

He'd heard the word *family*, and in Gasper's Cove, that was accepted as a plausible justification for any unjustifiable meddling.

CHAPTER EIGHT

Jimmy opened the door to the electrical box on the wall in the basement and whistled.

"Good thing you called me," he said. "There's no way what you got in here could handle the load."

"See?" Duck said, arms crossed over his broad chest. "Told you so. Old wiring needs an upgrade. Dangerous, am I right?"

"Could be." Jimmy bent down to cut wire from the coil on the concrete floor. He had lined up his tools close to the wall, so no one would trip on them. In his overalls and tool belt over a waffle-knit shirt, he looked neat and efficient, a younger version of Stuart, a reminder of my own sons. "But we can take care of it," he smiled at me. "Don't feel bad, I've seen worse. You should see Terry's cottage."

"Right, Sparky mentioned some kind of sewing operation?" I asked, still annoyed I had not heard about this through my usual channels. "Hard to get something like that going." Textile manufacturing in Nova Scotia had long ago moved offshore.

"I don't know," Jimmy said, peeling back some of the covering from the end of the wire, his moves practiced. "Terry figures he can make it work with the money he'll save on taxes and tariffs. Like that guy who died said."

"Nunn?" I asked.

"Yeah. He thought it up. Terry says he pays 20 percent to bring in those kilts because they are adult clothing. But Nunn pointed out that fabric comes in duty-free." Jimmy separated the smaller wires he'd exposed and picked up a pair of pliers. "Sharper than he looks, old Terry. He got it right away. Now he's saying if he can make the stuff here, he'll save a fortune."

"Have you heard who will do the sewing?" I pressed him. I wondered if this was why Murray Nunn had been interested in the Crafters.

"No clue," Jimmy said, "but I think he's got that covered. Sheila might know."

Sheila? The area's long-time kilt maker? What else did I not know? Sheila Mackenzie would get a call from me.

Duck stepped in front of me to watch Jimmy work. "I see what you're doing," he said to the electrician. "Appreciate you coming in."

"Oh, I don't mind being here on a Saturday." Jimmy reached for another tool. "Kind of nice to do a job on my own, no supervisor. And it gives me a break from cabling."

Duck snorted. He knew what Jimmy meant, though I didn't.

"Sounds like Sparky's busy," I continued, ignoring the inside joke. "Jobs here on the island and over in Drummond. What do you do for him, mostly?"

"General contracting," Jimmy said, focused on his work. "And other stuff that I fit in when I can."

"Oh yeah," said Duck, "how's that going?"

Jimmy picked up a drill. "The warranty work?" He looked sideways at me as he explained. "It's our sideline. Sparky brings in returns, and we refurbish them. Snap in a new board, tighten up the wires. Some of the stuff we get is in rough shape." Jimmy caught himself and stopped.

This was my opening.

"You mean appliances, like space heaters?" I asked innocently. "The same as the ones we had at the show? It was cold in there."

Jimmy bent down and carefully laid a screwdriver in his toolbox, turning it around so it would be where it belonged, next in order of size.

"Yes," he said, slowly. "Those."

Duck raised his eyebrows at me. He knew I was up to something.

I ignored him.

"I guess they have you bring in heaters until the crowds arrive and warm the place up," I kept going. "Then you go around and collect them." I took a chance. "I saw you go back to the booth after they took Murray away." Jimmy went still, listening to me. "I thought you mentioned you'd left by then?"

There. I'd said it.

Duck reached down, picked up Shadow.

"Later, buddy," he said to Jimmy. He and the cat went up the stairs to the main floor. Whatever I was up to, he wanted no part of it.

Jimmy waited until Duck was out of earshot before he spoke.

"I did go, like I said. But then, I remembered the heaters. I wanted to check, make sure there wasn't a problem in something I'd worked on. I had to go back."

Jimmy didn't look me in the eye when he said this. I had lots of experience with male evasiveness. I'd brought up two boys. There was more to this story.

"Okay." I waited. "I understand. Anything else?" I knew how to do this. Wait long enough to make a male uncomfortable, and he wouldn't be able to stand it. He would share the rest of the story just to escape.

Jimmy ran a microfiber cloth over the surface of his red toolbox. This was not a person who would forget much.

"There was one thing," he said. "That heater wasn't one of ours, not one I'd worked on. I realized that when I got back to the shop and had a better look at it. But I'd seen it before."

"You had? Where?"

"In the next booth. You know, where the food lady was."

"Moira?" I asked. "From the Salt Box?"

"Yeah, that's her," Jimmy said. "The one handing out the shortbread with the twigs in it."

"Summer savory?"

"Is that what it was? Got stuck in my teeth."

When it was clear Jimmy had nothing else to tell, I left him to his circuits and went upstairs to the main floor of the store.

"Get what you wanted?" Duck asked.

Nothing got by our handyman, except maybe his criminal brothers.

"You mean wiring? So we can keep the lights on? Sure."

Duck stood silently and looked at me. In his arms, Shadow nuzzled his cheek. Duck was as good at waiting for information as I was.

"Look. I saw Jimmy take out a space heater from under a table near where Murray collapsed. I wanted to ask him about it."

My words sounded interfering and accusatory, even to me. I thought I saw a flash of annoyance on Duck's face. There is only so much anyone can hide behind one cat.

"Don't go making something out of nothing." Duck was testy. "No one is more careful than that guy. Or more responsible. You should see his sweaters. There's easy Aran, and there's hard Aran. Jimmy does the hard."

I stared at Duck. "Jimmy knits?"

"Yes, I thought you knew. He's the one that got me into the club."

Duck put Shadow down and pulled up his pant leg. There, above the top of his steel-toed pull-on boot, I saw the rows of rust, ocher, and green.

Two women customers from Drummond appeared out of a side aisle. They bent down to admire Duck's ankles.

"Fair isle?" one asked. "You did that yourself?"

"Sure did," Duck said, with more pride than I had ever heard from him. "Some of the boys helped me. I was having a terrible time with the gusset." He pulled his pant leg down. "I picked up a few tips at the club. It's better now I'm doing toe-up."

"The club?" I asked, still stunned. I tried to imagine Duck's big hands holding four tiny needles.

"Yeah, I thought you knew. Men with Sticks. We get together once a week and knit at the church. Charity work, mostly."

"They're famous," one of the Drummond women interjected. "Newborn hats, vests for rescue chickens, and cuddle blankets for the animal shelter."

"That's right," the woman beside her nodded. She had seed packets and a garage sale sign in her hands, two signs of spring. "The ladies' auxiliary collects yarn for them," she added.

"You got it," Duck said. "We try to do useful stuff. I learned how to knit from my granddad; he picked it up when he was, you know, away for a bit."

I had no reason to be surprised by this. Traditionally, Highland men knit. The women were the spinners. The patterns on pullovers in those days were sometimes passed down through families. I could also imagine, in the case of Duck's grandfather, that incarceration would lend itself to a contained craft like knitting. But how was it possible I was only hearing about this side of Duck's life now?

I didn't know what to say and didn't have a chance. Outside in the back parking lot, a horn blared, once and then twice.

"Oh, there we go," Duck said, listening. "That tourist bunch. Probably wondering where to park."

"Right. Off you go then," I said. I had forgotten about the tour bus. We were the last stop on the island before Drummond and an overnight stay at the Anchor Motel. "I better get up to the Co-Op and open the cash."

I left Duck to greet the tourists. The two spring shoppers disappeared into aisle four, one of them with her cell phone out. I made my way to the staircase to the second floor. Colleen was waiting for me.

"Here," she said, handing me a zippered pouch. "The float. Coins and cash. Canadian and American. You're going to need it."

I took the bag. "Did you know that Duck knits?" I asked her.

"Sure. Everybody does."

"Did you know Jimmy knits?"

"Of course. Ganseys and Aran," she answered. "He's the president of the club."

I deflated. I was the manager of nothing. But I made one last try.

"Have you heard any news about Sheila Mackenzie?"

"The kilts, or the work she's doing for Terry?"

Where had I been? "She is working for him?"

"She might be," Colleen said. "Most of the other women around here are too busy."

I felt on firmer ground. "No kidding, the Co-op's doing well."

Colleen looked at me oddly. "There's that, but I'm thinking more of those sewing for that woman who was in here the other day. The thin one, in the boots."

I had trouble keeping up with all that I didn't know.

"Who?"

"That designer who's buying up the quilts. You know the one." Colleen leaned in. "Apparently, she's got them making sample garments. Just a few seams in some old quilts, but she seems to think it's a big deal. Not that you heard it from me. Promise?"

"Sure, but why promise?" Outside, I could hear the wave of tourists advancing across the parking lot; in a minute, they would be inside. "Why am I not supposed to know this?"

Colleen looked toward the back door. "Well, you wouldn't, if I didn't have a big mouth. So, don't let on. She had the girls sign some kind of confidentiality agreement, whatever that is. They are supposed to do the sewing and say they haven't." She shook her head. "You wonder what kind of world these people live in, don't you? Where sewing is a secret?"

I didn't have to wonder. I knew.

CHAPTER NINE

After I had sold the visitors enough place mats, tea cozies, and wind chimes to sink a battleship, I went down to my manager's office and put on the kettle.

There was a handwritten note on my desk from Duck.

Call Sheila Mackenzie.

I dropped a Morse's tea bag in the store's teapot and dialed her number.

"Colleen says you want to talk to me," Sheila said. "Sorry I was slow to get back to you. This is my day for pleating."

I didn't remember deputizing Colleen to set up a meeting with the local kilt maker, but since she had, I made the best of it.

"Right, we do a lot in the Co-op with the tourists. I am interested in anything being made in the area. Wondering how the kilts are doing." This was vague, and I had no idea what to say next.

But I had said enough for Sheila.

"Look," she said. "I've been at it all morning. I could use a break. Why don't you come out for tea?"

"Do you mind?"

"Not at all," Sheila said. "There are things going on, and it is better you hear about them from me."

Sheila lived in one of the older homes in Gasper's Cove, built in the last century by a sea captain. It was tall, dark, and narrow, like many homes of its era on the island. There was elaborate carving around the eaves and the windows, and high, in the middle of the roof, a single glass room like an unlit lighthouse, a "widow's walk" built for pacing, worrying, and watching the horizon for boats that would never return.

The front door was thick with generational layers of paint and a weather-pitted brass knocker shaped like an anchor. I raised it and let it fall. While I waited for the door to open, I thought of what Colleen had told me. Were some of our quilters and sewers doing production work? Sheila would know. She would tell me.

The door pulled open. And there she was.

Sheila Mackenzie hadn't changed in forty years. She had the ageless look of someone who was living exactly the life she wanted. Her face was unlined, marked only with tiny red veins broken by the weather. Her sandy hair curled in the rows she cultivated every night with foam rollers. I was sure her closet contained nothing but pleated skirts, white Oxford cloth blouses, and lambswool cardigans, because I had never seen her wear anything else. Her only accessories were a large man's watch, a Celtic cross around her neck, and a measuring tape draped over her shoulders. She wore lace-up shoes and always, in every season, navy knee socks.

When Sheila Mackenzie found what she wanted, she stuck with it.

"How are you?" I asked as I crossed the threshold into the workroom that was the kilt maker's living room.

"Busy," she said. "Highland dance competitions are coming up." Her arms swept over the two oak ping-pong-size tables covered with bolts of tartan, and lengths, 8 yards a kilt, laid out and half pleated. Sheila's kilts were done in the classic style, to the "sett," following the pattern repeats of the different colored threads used to weave the tartan. Although slower to do than modern measurement methods, and consuming more fabric, kilts done by the sett created a continuity of design so that the pleats on both the front and the back of the kilt looked exactly the same.

"My goodness, such beautiful work," I said. "How many pleats?"

"Depends, doesn't it? On the size of the wearer—25, 34." Sheila ran a gentle hand over a blue, green, and black MacKay tartan. "This one will need the full 34."

"That looks almost like the Nova Scotia tartan," I said.

"Almost, but not quite." Sheila gave the wool a soft pat, as if reassuring it that she would be back to it soon. "A couple of differences. This is MacKay, a real clan tartan. The province's tartan got made up. It's not really authentic."

"Not authentic?" I loved being in this room, with the tools, bolts and bolts of fabrics, two large gravity-fed irons, presses, and industrial straight-stitch sewing machines. I knew that somewhere in the back of the house was a kitchen, and upstairs a bedroom. But Sheila's life was lived in this room.

I pulled myself back into our conversation. "Our province's official tartan is a fake?"

"A well-meaning one," Sheila corrected. "Just another weaver thinking on the spot. Don't you know the story?"

"No, I don't, tell me."

"Alright then. 1953. Bessie Bailey Murray had to do a banner for the Nova Scotia Sheep Breeders Association booth at the Farm and Fisheries exhibition in Truro."

"You mean the show they have every year?"

"Exactly the same. But you know how they fight." Sheila said. "It was a real problem."

"Who fights?" I asked. "The sheep breeders?"

"Well, them, too, but that's another story. I mean the clans. Doesn't take much to set them off."

"Not following," I said. "How does that matter to a banner?"

"Everything," Sheila said. "Poor Bessie was supposed to weave in a landscape of a Nova Scotia highlander with his sheep, water in the background. The usual."

"And the problem was?"

The question startled Sheila. "Fellow was supposed to be wearing a kilt. Bessie was a weaver. But what tartan could she use that wouldn't set somebody off? I mean, you can't play favorites at the Truro Exhibition."

"True enough. So, what did she do?"

"Made one up. Invented one. Blue for the water, green for the woods, white for the surf, red for a bit of color, or a lion or something. Gold for the empire. The thing was, people went nuts. Loved it. Mary Black, the province's handicrafts director, saw it and got a scarf made up for the premier. The next thing you know, the province passed an act to protect it, make it illegal even to reproduce it without a license." Sheila pointed to several bolts of Nova Scotia tartan on her shelf. "The real thing is important in my world," she said, reaching out to touch her pleats, her fingers folding the next one as if out of genetic muscle memory, a motion she could make in the dark.

I watched her. Sheila was her craft. "That's a lot of fabric," I noted, with a true sewer's fabric envy. I reached over and felt it. The quality wool, alive between my fingers, was closer in spirit to the fields than to the loom. "Where do you get it?"

"Direct from Scotland, suppliers I've used for years. But this"—she swept an arm over the tables—"Terry brought back for me."

Terry. We were back to the reason for my visit.

"Oh, yes," I said, trying to fake nonchalance. "I hear he's setting up some sort of sewing operation. Am I going to lose some of my Crafters to him? Or to that Louise Haggerty?"

"Oh, you know about that," Sheila said. "There might be some girls doing some work for both of them on the side. They probably didn't tell you in case you got worried that they were bailing on you. But listen, don't panic. Piecework gets old pretty quickly. They won't last."

"What do you mean?"

"Sewing is too hard if you don't love it," Sheila said. "That's why I usually never work for anyone else. I like to take my time, give each of my kilts the attention they deserve, talk to them. Sure, some things you do for money, but only to support what you love. Like Terry and his tartans. A means to an end."

"What do you mean?"

"He loves his history, Terry does. If he could make his money doing genealogy, that's all he would do. But there aren't enough Moiras around."

"You mean people who'll hire him to research the family tree? I heard about that. Surprised me. I thought she already knew everything about her background. The *Hector* and all that. She's built her business around it."

"You mean she's built her business *on* it," Sheila corrected. "Terry found a long-lost relative on her mother's side, not even one of the Frasers, no family, recently deceased. Terry proved the connection, and Moira got her inheritance. She would never have had the money for the restaurant without it."

"It pays to know your past, I guess."

Sheila sniffed. "The parts that are true. Some aren't. No wonder the lighting is bad in that place," she added.

I was lost. "What place?"

"That overpriced restaurant in that old basement." Sheila picked up a long wooden ruler. I could tell she was ready to go back to work. "Did you have a good look at that fabric she's got framed on the walls?"

"You mean the tartan that came over with the family on the first ship?" I knew the Fraser tartan and wool. Everything looked genuine to me.

"Did you get a closeup of the threads?" Sheila asked, a woman whose professional life was spent doing just that. "Or was it too dark in there?"

I didn't understand. "I was there for dinner ... "

"You should carry a flashlight in your purse like I do, helps me find things." A memory agitated Sheila. She tapped her ruler on the edge of her oak worktable. "Perfectly even threads both ways in those pieces she's got framed. I got suspicious when I saw the weave in that wool. The spacing was too even; old looms couldn't do that. Wool then didn't have the lanolin worked out of it. There was no way to spin it or weave it that evenly. And you know what that means?"

I shook my head.

"No way that tartan on the walls was handwoven. And if it made its way to Nova Scotia, it would have been on an airplane, not on the *Hector*."

"Are you saying you think Moira's lying about her history? What about the dead relative?"

"Well, they're dead, aren't they?" Sheila pointed out. "We'll never know. But I can tell you one thing: Any person who will lie about a family tartan will lie about anything."

CHAPTER TEN

That evening, after my sewing class, I reflected on the inauthentic proprietor of an authentic Scottish restaurant. If Sheila was right about her thread count, and it was likely she was, other aspects of Moira Fraser might not be what they seemed.

I wondered what those could be. Lost in my ruminations, a discreet cough made me look up. Heidi was outside the doorway.

"Awesome class tonight," she said, tentatively stepping back into the classroom. At the top of her tote bag, I saw the edge of the binder she'd made for my handouts, sectioned with tabs and color coded. No one tried harder than Heidi, or was as worried about making a mistake. "Need any help cleaning up? Empty the iron? Sweep?"

"Thanks, but I'm nearly done." One of that night's students had left behind a pattern piece for a sleeve. I put it away in a drawer to return to them the next class. "Come in and talk to me while I finish up," I suggested." Your project is going great, by the way. You're a natural."

The praise lit up Heidi's face. I wondered how often she was told she was good at what she did, or how often anyone noticed.

"I like sewing, I really do. It makes me feel like myself. I think about these classes all week." Heidi bent down and picked up a tangle of bobbin thread on the floor I had missed. "My job's not exactly creative."

I pulled shards of fabric from the bristles of the broom and emptied the dustbin. "I can see that. Mind you, I've never been an executive, or anybody's, assistant. What do you do, apart from making appointments, I mean?"

"Well, according to my job description, I am there to support the work of the council as the mayor sees fit." Heidi laughed, but without humor. "Translated, that means doing whatever Mr. Clarke doesn't want to do himself."

"Which is?"

"Listening to upset constituents and calming them down before he has to deal with them." Her own honesty seemed to startle her. "And other regular stuff, like I said last class. Setting up meetings, making agendas, screening the mayor's calls."

"That sounds like a lot of variety," I offered. I couldn't see that it would be a lot of fun working with our mayor. He was an officious man, the kind who enjoyed making rules just because he could. As far as I could make out, he spent most of his time trying to control the random activities of the people of Gasper's Cove and Drummond and then avoiding these same people when they protested.

"Do you enjoy it?" I asked.

Heidi walked over to a table and sat down. She picked up a foot pedal off the floor and wrapped the electrical cord around it.

"Mostly," she said after a pause. "Honestly, he's not such a bad boss, but he can be a stickler. If you work for him, you have to pay attention to the details. I think that's because he used to work for the province before he came here. You know, like it's hard for him to scale down, to forget he used to swim in a bigger pond."

This was a thoughtful observation. Heidi noticed people. I'd remember that.

"That makes sense," I said. "And it would explain all those notices he's put up. Telling us what we already know." I was sure our mayor was not aware of how his excessive signage amused the citizens of the municipality. "Library" twenty feet from a building with that very word carved in stone over the entrance. "Children Playing" next to the swings at the park and "Pedestrian Pathway" beside sidewalks.

Heidi groaned. "Tell me about it. You should hear the waste-of-my-tax-dollars calls. If he's going to spend money, he has to show he has it."

"Darlene thinks the same thing," I said. "Was that why Mr. Nunn was here?" I realized I was prying, but I had promised Stuart I'd get him information. Heidi would know any backstory.

"Yes, poor guy. He was in the office a few days before he died. I think the mayor knew him from before—you know, when he worked in the city. I got the impression Mr. Nunn's main thing was to look for places with businesses that qualified for government money. Then, when he found them, he'd submit proposals for economic development funding from the province and the feds. Start-up capital, seed money, he called it." Heidi finished her foot-pedal wrapping and bent down to the floor to pick up pins a more reckless sewer had dropped.

"I don't understand," I said. "The council doesn't have money to give out. It mainly needs the money. Why would Nunn contact the mayor?"

"To get his help," Heidi explained. "The province will only fund projects that have municipal support and won't violate any local regulations."

"Regulations?"

Heidi clasped her hands in front of her on the sewing table like it was a desk. Unconsciously, the tone of her voice shifted into bureaucratic mode. She might not like all her job, but I could see she was good at it. "You have no idea. There are regulations for just about everything in the Maritimes. A lot of them make no sense, and no one remembers why they were written. For example, do you know it's illegal to paint a wood ladder in Nova Scotia?"

"I did not. Why?"

"In case the paint is hiding structural weakness. Can't be too careful."

"Makes sense. Sort of."

"And how about this one? In Prince Edward Island, it is illegal to build a snowman taller than 30 inches. Wonder who enforces that? A bunch of little boys? And in Halifax, you are not allowed to drive a taxi while wearing a T-shirt. Keeping it classy. But New Brunswick is worse. There, you can't get away with anything."

"Like what?"

"In New Brunswick, it's illegal to walk around in public with a reptile around your neck."

"You're kidding."

"I am not. Must have been a big problem. It had to stop."

I laughed. "What about locally? Any strange by-laws?"

"No," Heidi said. "We're pretty dull. No snake patrols. Around here, it is all about the water. Keeping sailors out of fishing areas. Telling boat owners, without exceptions, they need a permit to put in a mooring."

The mention of sailors triggered something Stuart had said. I couldn't remember what that was. "Exceptions?" I asked. "Moorings?"

"Because moorings are anchored below the natural waterline, they count as underwater structures," Heidi recited, sounding like she was reading from a manual. "You can't put them in anywhere—not in a designated fishing area or anywhere along the shore. Unless you have an exemption, what they call an exception."

"And that would be?"

"A sort of permit to ignore the rule. Something a property owner can get because of the 60-meter rule." Heidi spoke with the singsong tone of someone who explained this a lot. "Anyone who owns coastal property can moor a boat in the water opposite, without a permit, as long as it's not in a fishing area and no farther than 60 meters out. One mooring per property."

That was it. I felt the flash.

The sparks in my head connected, attaching this discussion to Stuart's Sail By mystery. This was why locals had lost public access to the land they had traditionally visited to see the boat parade go past.

"Any property?" I asked, to make sure. "Even tiny random pieces of municipal land?"

"Yes," Heidi said. "One advantage to acquiring property like that would be to secure an unregistered mooring."

My mind was off to a race of my own, chasing ideas. Who would need a mooring like that? Summer sailors? Tourism operators? Casual fishermen?

Who else? Most of that land was too rocky to build anything larger than a shed.

A shed?

A shed.

Metal in the walls. Nancy's story. Rumrunners. Smugglers. Imports and exports.

I sat down in the chair next to Heidi. My careening thoughts made me unsteady.

"So, someone might buy up land up around Shore Road, raggedy bits of useless land, just for the mooring?"

"It's a possibility." Heidi stood and picked up her tote bag.

I couldn't help myself. "Do you know anything about Saltire Investments?"

Heidi shrugged. "I recognize the name. I saw it on some deeds, and I remember thinking it reminded me of the flag."

"Saltire? Are you sure? But who are they?" I asked. Wait until Stuart heard all this.

"I wondered that myself, so I asked the mayor." Heidi opened the bobbin case of the sewing machine in front of her and pulled out a trapped thread. "Loose ends bother me," she explained.

"What did he say?"

"Well, if the mayor knew I told you this, I would be in trouble, but since I don't have any names, I can't see the harm." Heidi leaned in closer, pushing the machine back, as if she were afraid it would listen. "The mayor said that when Mr. Nunn came in and asked to purchase these orphan pieces of land—that's what we call them—he jumped at the chance. And because they were such small parcels of property, it took no time to get the sales approved quickly, one at a time. The mayor told me no one would even notice we'd sold them."

No one but Stuart Campbell, I thought.

"Murray Nunn was Saltire Investments?" The man involved in these unusual transactions was now dead. "He was the buyer?"

"Not directly," Heidi reached forward and snapped the door to the machine's bobbin-area shut. "Look. I heard something I shouldn't have one time when I took in coffee. Sometimes, they treat me like a waitress. Anyway, they stopped talking as soon as I came into the room, but I am sure I heard Mr. Nunn tell Mayor Elliot that Saltire was one of his clients."

"Who is Saltire?"

Heidi picked up her tote bag. She seemed flustered, ready to leave. "No idea," she said. "Stupid me. I shouldn't have said anything. If the mayor found out I was gossiping like this, I might lose my job."

I put a hand on Heidi's arm.

"Don't worry," I said. "I won't tell anyone. Done. Forgotten."

Heidi's shoulders relaxed, reassured.

I'd made a promise, and I would not break it.

I'd keep what she had told me to myself.

But forget it, I would not.

After Heidi left, I walked back to my office to think. Toby was there, waiting for me. During the day, he hosted the front entrance, but on class nights, he retreated to the back of the store to nap.

Toby stopped gnawing his yak milk bone when I walked in.

"Well, you'll never guess what I found out," I told him.

Toby gave me a dog shrug and went back to his bone. Heidi had told me exactly what Stuart wanted to know. Now, all I had to do was find out which of Murray Nunn's clients had bought that land in a way that wouldn't implicate Heidi. Then, I could tell Stuart everything.

I picked up my keys and told Toby we were going home.

I knew what to do. I'd go visiting tomorrow.

I suspected that there was more than designer jackets under construction in Gasper's Cove.

CHAPTER ELEVEN

I waited until Catherine was halfway through her souvlaki before I asked my question. I'd planned to go out to the Inn for a chat, but she asked instead if we could meet in town for lunch. Since leaving her library career to be a co-owner of a bed-and-breakfast, Catherine didn't have many lunches she didn't serve herself.

We began by sharing local gossip. Then, I moved in to gather facts.

Catherine was good on facts.

I looked out of the window of the Agapi restaurant and watched the beginning of the tourist season drive by.

"Lots of Ontario plates this year," I said, easing into where I wanted to go. I picked up some pita bread and scooped up some distraction tzatziki. "Hey, didn't you live in Toronto for a while?"

Catherine smiled at the memory. She'd dressed up for lunch, trading in her quilted innkeeper vest for a denim skirt and a floral Liberty print blouse. "That I did. It's where I got my master's. I worked there for a while in reference, at

Osgoode Hall Law School. Only for a summer. The project was a bibliography of Canadian legal references. That was the old days. We worked from the card catalogue for the older publications, those beautiful oak cabinets ...," she sighed. "I learned a lot about the law."

"Bet you did." I pretended to be fascinated by the cubes of feta on my plate. "Listen, I was watching the news." I was making this up, but since the news covered everything, I thought it was safe. "Something about NDAs. What can you tell me about them?"

Catherine put down her napkin. It was as if she had been waiting for someone to ask this exact question. Or about anything that had once warranted a bibliographical entry.

"That's a huge topic," she said. "I'm not surprised you've heard about them. There's been a certain amount of abuse with how they've been used. That's why so many are being challenged in the courts."

"Tell me more," I said. Silently, I wondered how I would steer this conversation back to orphan land moorings and production sewing. It would not be easy.

"NDAs, nondisclosure agreements—most people would know them as confidentiality agreements—are meant to protect things the law considers of financial value. Your reputation as a public person, for example, or, more often, confidential information, anything that would cause you financial loss if a competitor found out about it."

"That makes sense," I said. "What can be wrong with that?"

"Think about it." Catherine cut up her pita bread. I had torn mine. "Sometimes, they can be used to hide secrets, in the worst cases, from people who trust you. Part of the point is that in a self-regulated society, they shouldn't be necessary." She swiped her pita through her taramosalata. "Most of us keep things to ourselves out of decency or because of professional ethics—doctors, lawyers, the clergy, for example."

I stabbed the last tomato in my Greek salad. The oregano in the dressing was fresh. It made me think of Moira and her summer savory shortbread. It was important to know what belonged where.

"Have you ever signed a confidentiality agreement, an NDA?" I asked.

"No, I haven't," Catherine said. "But many public servants do. It depends on whether they have access to financial information. Like so much in the law, it all comes down to money and protecting value and property. Reputational, intellectual, and physical."

George Kosoulas ambled toward our table.

"Anything else you ladies would like?" he asked as he picked up our empty plates.

"Oh, no, thanks. I've eaten more than I should have," Catherine said. "But I wouldn't mind your mother's recipe for that dip."

George laughed. "You're not the only customer who asks. There's lots who'd kill to know what's in it. But she won't even tell me. Trade secret," he said with a wink. "Know what I mean?"

We did.

Out on the sidewalk, I walked Catherine to her car. On the way, we discussed the upcoming tourist season at the Inn, Catherine's spring-cleaning list, and her ongoing struggle with Rollie, who wanted to upgrade the decor.

"He doesn't get it," she said. "The Inn's windows rattle. We are right next to the winds of the North Atlantic. Century-old floorboards are supposed to creak. Clean is enough. New is not necessary. Buildings are like books. Sometimes the best ones are a little musty." She stopped with one hand on her car door. "It was nice to go out for lunch, but I'm afraid to turn my back on him these days. He wants to put down laminate flooring and put up vinyl siding, for practical reasons. Do you believe that?"

"Oh, he wouldn't do that," I said. "Rollie has more sense."

"About some things, yes," Catherine said. "But sometimes, he can be such a man. Look at that stunt he pulled with the beds."

I looked across at the boats bobbing in the waves. Rollie was my cousin; we were standing in public. This was uncomfortable.

"Not sure what you mean," I said carefully. "Do I want to know?"

Catherine rolled her eyes. "I'm talking about quilts. The vintage ones we had on the single beds. That woman from New York is staying with us and she talked him into selling them to her. And he did! He made a deal with her to exchange them for something from Amazon. Wash and wear. Wrinkle-free! *Reproductions.*" Catherine said the last word like a curse. "Our guests expect wrinkles, they expect wear. How can he not get that?"

No wonder Catherine was upset. I knew what *wrinkle-free* meant. Polyester. Likely batting, maybe even the fabric.

I shuddered.

So, now Louise Haggerty was scavenging not only my crafters but also the quilts from local beds. I had to know more about her. How would I do that?

The answer was right in front of me, full of souvlaki and secret-recipe tzatziki.

"Catherine, you still have those research skills?"

I immediately knew I had offended my almost-cousin-in-law.

"What are you talking about?" she said. "Librarianship is like riding a bike, but more important." She assessed me like I was still one of her patrons at the Gasper's Cove library. "Is there anything I can help you find?" she asked from memory.

"You have no idea," I said. I had far more questions between my ears than I had answers. Where would I start? "But there are two things I wouldn't mind checking out." Catherine's face was alert. If she were a dog, right now she would be a fox terrier, ears up. "If you have the time," I added, thinking of the spring cleaning.

"I do," Catherine said briskly, "and I am as fast as I am good. Hang on a minute." Catherine pulled out a new spiral-bound notebook from her bag. She slapped it on the hood of her car, opened it to the first, and blank, page, and clicked the top of a pen. "What are your search terms?"

She wrote 1.0 in the margin of the lined sheet and looked up at me, waiting.

This was more than I had expected, but exactly what I needed.

"Alrighty then. Louise Haggerty. Her company's called Re-Creations. Sustainable something or other. Based in New York, Montreal, Toronto, and some other place. She says she's a designer. My question is, is she? If so, what does that look like? Apart from buying old textiles and quilts from small communities, hiring local women to do the sewing, and then reselling them for a fortune." I watched Catherine take notes. Either her handwriting was unexpectedly messy, like mine, or she was taking shorthand, a skill I hadn't seen in action in more than 30 years. I held up my fingers, my version of organizing my thoughts. "I would like to know her background. And"—I had to think about how to express this—"why did she come all the way to this little place to do whatever she does? We're not exactly on the map. At least, none she would have."

Catherine smiled as she scribbled. Obviously, she was having more fun working on the hood of her car than she had had anywhere in a long time. "That all on this one?" she asked.

"One other thing." I had to be careful and protect my indiscreet aunt. "Why would she want to keep what she's doing, particularly with the sewers, a secret? I don't know if you can find that out, but it would be interesting."

Catherine sniffed. "Like I said when we were having lunch, these things somehow always come down to money. I'll see what I can uncover." She wrote herself another line of hieroglyphics, then stopped, her pen poised over the page. "You said there were two things?"

"Right. This may have nothing to do with Louise, but I have a hunch it might. There is an investment company called Saltire. They've bought a bit of land around here." I had to think of a reason to ask this. "It has to do with Stuart's Sail By at the yacht club, and people who want to get close to the water to see it. I'd like to know who they are, or at least what other things they have invested in. Maybe in New York? Montreal? Toronto? Or that other place?"

Catherine wrote this down beside the number 2.0.

"Hmm, *saltire*?" she asked. "As in the flags? St. Andrew's Cross?"

"I guess so," I said. "That's the only saltire I've ever heard of."

"Same here," Catherine said, popping her notebook and pen back in her bag, ready to begin her assignment. "Whatever the connection, it's got to be Scottish. I'll start there."

CHAPTER TWELVE

I stood at the sink the next morning and thought about history. The Rankins, like every family in Gasper's Cove, had their share of it. Some of it came from Scotland, when the Highland Clearances loaded families onto boats and pushed away from ancestral shores. Some had survived in stories, repeated at every Thanksgiving, Christmas, or Easter table. But even more of our history had traveled through the generations hidden in our blood. Not passed on through genetics, but more mysteriously, expressed as predispositions or, with our family, as the ability to feel premonitions.

I felt one now, as if the past were trying to reach me. Catherine had gone looking for evidence, but I wasn't sure if what mattered had been recorded. As I hand washed my breakfast dishes, I strained to connect with the sense that something significant was about to happen, but the feeling shimmered where I couldn't reach it and then was gone. Frustrated, I put my Royal Doulton teacup and plate in the drying rack and the big brown teapot I had inherited in the cupboard. I was careful with that pot. It had belonged to a great-grandmother who once had run back into the flames of a house fire to save it. That act of courage was both brave and foolish, a combination my family remembered, understood, and admired.

The wall phone rang.

"I heard," Nancy said. "It's all over town. When did you know?"

"Know what?" I put my tea towel down and sat down on a chrome-legged kitchen chair. I looked at the clock. It was 7:30 in the morning. A time only someone who had been stewing all night would call.

"That Murray Nunn died because Jimmy MacNeil made a mistake." I listened to Nancy pause to sip her tea. I suspected ours was not her first conversation of the morning. "Sparky's let him go. That's got to be why. You've killed someone, you've killed someone, if you meant to or not. Know what I mean?"

"That's crazy," I said. "Who in the world told you that?"

"You did."

"Me? What are you talking about? Nancy, I haven't seen you since the show."

All over town?

"Well, not *told* told, but good as. Eleanor heard you, and she called Marion, and Marion called me." Nancy seemed to think this explained everything.

"Who is Eleanor, and who is Marion?"

"Maybe you don't know them. They are sisters, from over the way. It was their nephew, the really short one, not a lot of hair, but with a very good job at the Foodmart, who I fixed up with Louise, from Bridgewater. You know, the girl whose dad shows the oxen? Anyway, lovely couple. Two kids now, another on the way ... "

"Stop, Nancy. Right there. I didn't talk to any two sisters, and I didn't say a thing about Jimmy. You've got it all wrong."

Nancy's indignation flowed down the phone line. "I think not. I am repeating what you said yourself yesterday about Jimmy. Eleanor heard every word, and so she called me. She knows I've been working on a girl for him. She thought I'd want the information before I set him up. You know, no job anymore, maybe killed someone. Not looking like such a good prospect."

I let Nancy talk while I thought back to when Jimmy was at the store. An image came to mind. Two women had walked into my conversation with Duck, admired his socks, and then gone off down aisle four. Eleanor and Marion? One with her phone out, talking. Had I said anything they misunderstood?

I had. And I knew what it was.

I had told Duck that Jimmy had gone back for a heater that had been plugged in where Murray had been standing. I had meant it as a description of an event that had made me curious, not as an accusation. But that is what the two sisters, with a short, bald, now happily married nephew, had thought. And now, so did the whole community. Was this why Jimmy had lost his job? Because of something I had said? Should I talk to Sparky? What would I say?

No, the person I had to talk to first was Jimmy's uncle. Stuart.

I cut Nancy off, right in the middle of a description of her inbox of unattached rural Nova Scotia singles.

"Look, Nancy. I have to go. What your friends thought they heard didn't mean what they thought. I'll straighten this up. Talk to you later, okay?"

"You do that," Nancy said. "And any updates on Jimmy, please let me know. I got a couple of girls who might be interested in him anyway. Not girls really, more like older women, not a lot of options. But the kind who might turn a man around. He seems like such a nice guy."

"Yes, he is," I assured her. "And he didn't deserve any of this."

For the first time since we'd met, Stuart didn't want to talk to me.

"Not now, Valerie."

"Why not?"

"I'm busy," he answered.

"When will you not be busy?"

Stuart's voice was distant. Detached. Like he was someone else.

"No idea. Look, not now."

"Wait, wait. I know Sparky let Jimmy go. If it had something to do with what I said, it was a mistake. It was those sisters. In aisle four. They don't know what they are talking about. Nancy got their nephew married off. So what? That's no reason to listen to them."

"Valerie, I don't know what you are talking about. I don't have time to find out. This doesn't concern you." Stuart sounded like an elementary school principal, not like a romantic interest. "Like I said, we're busy. Got to go."

"Who's 'we'? Who are you with? Where are you?"

"Jimmy and me, we're with the RCMP. Waiting to talk to Officer Corkum. Goodbye."

I stared at my phone. Stuart had hung up on me. I would have to go over to Drummond and track him down.

When I saw Stuart next, he and Jimmy were walking out of the RCMP detachment in Drummond. It had been a hurried drive over the causeway, and I was on my way to Stuart's house when I passed them. Shocked to see them still there, I cut across two lanes and pulled into the Mounties' parking lot to talk.

The young electrician looked different today. I realized I'd rarely seen him out of his work overalls, but this morning he was dressed in a zip-up navy jacket and jeans. As he walked beside his uncle, I saw the same stride in them both, as if Jimmy and Stuart were two different editions of the same story. Genetically reliable.

I got out of my car and intercepted them. When he saw me, Jimmy paused. I felt him withdraw into himself. He nodded to me politely, because that's what Campbells did, but didn't say anything. I didn't detect the same air of hurt in Stuart, but I felt his annoyance as it rolled to me. He stopped on the pavement and waved his nephew away.

"You go along," he said. "I'll call you later. I'm going to have a word with Valerie here."

Jimmy muttered thanks to his uncle and then strode off to his truck, his back rigid with mannered confidence, in case anyone he knew drove by and saw he'd been with the RCMP.

I stepped forward. "Stuart, let me explain."

"We can't do this here," he said. "Meet me at the house."

Was this a good or a bad thing? I wondered. "Okay, but before that, I want to tell you something."

"It can wait. See you soon." Stuart turned and walked away, his posture like his nephew's.

Birdie met me at the door. The little Duck Toller, at least, was glad to see me. Stuart, there before me, was more reserved, no tail wagging or sloppy kisses from him.

"Come in," he said, holding the door open, but holding back what he had to say to me until I was in the house. "I'll put the kettle on. It's too early for lunch, but I've been up for hours. Feel like a sandwich? Chicken salad?"

"Definitely, love one." I followed Stuart into the kitchen. He wore the denim apron I'd made him last Christmas. This was a good sign. Also, I figured, you don't feed people if you are going to give up on them. I sat down at Stuart's sanded and waxed old oak table. Birdie positioned himself underneath at my feet. Small and red, with alert brown eyes, he looked like a fox, one waiting for anything edible to be dropped. I noticed two plates on the counter and four pieces of heavily seeded bread on the cutting board. I'd had these sandwiches before. I didn't know how Stuart did it. Every piece of chicken, celery, and apple chopped up fine, every tiny piece, the exact same size. He also always added Dijon and a little curry powder to the mayonnaise. I didn't put that much care into Sunday dinner, and we both knew it.

After the sandwiches were on the table, and I'd accepted Stuart's offer of a home-fermented dill pickle, I asked the most obvious question.

"Why were you and Jimmy at the RCMP?"

Stuart pushed his plate away and looked at me.

"Wade wanted to talk to Jimmy about what happened to Murray at the show. These days, there's software they use to take readings from pacemakers after a critical event. It helps identify device failure, and that matters. The results came back." Stuart reached under the table to feel for the reassurance of Birdie's head. He looked tired.

I held my breath. There was a reason I was hearing this. "What did the results say?"

"It confirmed what they thought: that a strong electrical interference had caused a malfunction in Murray's pacemaker. He had heart issues, so that's all it took." Stuart stood up and took his plate back to the counter. He wasn't going to eat his sandwich. I'd finished mine. If we'd been on better terms, I would have asked if I could wrap his up and take it home.

Stuart turned around. "And apparently, you told people you saw Jimmy removing electronics from the booth. Why would you say that?" Stuart wrapped up his plate in plastic wrap and put it where I couldn't reach it, in the fridge. "Why imply he'd done something suspicious? Why put that idea in people's heads? A man died, Valerie! You don't speculate about something like that. You did a lot of damage. You put Sparky in a corner. He had no choice but to let Jimmy go. That boy did nothing wrong. How do you think he feels right now?"

I opened my mouth to explain that the local rumor mill had embroidered my simple comment, then I stopped. There was no excuse that would help, and anything I said now would only make it worse.

"I'm so, so sorry," I offered, and then, because I couldn't help myself, I kept going, no sense to control my curiosity. "What happened with Wade?"

"Thanks to you, of course, he grilled Jimmy. I was there because I thought he needed someone with him," Stuart said this to Birdie, to keep from looking at me. "And Wade wanted him to bring in the heater so they could have a look at it and basically to hear what Jimmy had to say for himself."

"What did Jimmy tell him?" I asked quickly, which I knew was a mistake. "He told me he thought it had come from Moira's booth," I added.

"That's what he says. But I guess Wade called her, and she says she can't remember a heater at the show. So, it's her word against his." Stuart came back and sat at the table. "That's not the point. You've got to understand how Jimmy thinks. I do. He's a worrier. It runs in our family. He wanted to know if he'd done anything wrong before he said anything. That's why he dodged the question about when he'd left the arena. We'll just have to see what the RCMP does next, I guess."

"Oh, what a mess," I said. "What can I do?"

"Nothing," Stuart answered. "Look. I know how your mind works, how you get all these strange ideas, but what hurts is that you didn't talk any of this over with me first. Jimmy said you more or less accused him of being up to something. Where was I in all of this? There's a lack of trust about this that doesn't make any sense to me. We're either together, or we're not. I don't know where we go from here," Stuart said as a statement of defeat.

I didn't know how to respond. There had to be a way to make this right.

"I'm going to fix this," I said, getting to my feet. "I'll do something. I have an idea. I'll figure it out."

Stuart turned away from me and reached down to Birdie.

"You don't get it, do you?" he said. "Not everything is up to you. And that's the problem."

CHAPTER THIRTEEN

Before I drove away, I sat in my car in front of Stuart's house and went through my purse. At the show, I was sure of it, Jeff had given me a card. I finally found it, stuck to the back of a semi-melted piece of lint-covered chocolate.

I didn't recognize the area code, but like so many cell numbers, it connected right away.

"Live Wire Communications," Jeff answered. His greeting matched the name on the card. I wondered if Jeff was the sole owner of this energetic-sounding enterprise or if he worked with anyone else.

"Hi, Jeff? Valerie Rankin. I don't know if you remember me from last weekend. You were in our booth, making a video for Moira from the Salt Box?" I felt more comfortable referring to Jeff's client, who was still alive and well, than to his associate, Murray Nunn, who was anything but.

"Ah, Valerie, of course I remember you. You're the deputy mayor's cousin, aren't you?"

"Darlene? Yes, I am. Listen, this may seem like a strange request, but it might help out a friend of mine. How good was your video of the Salt Box booth?"

"It was good"—there was a hint of terseness in the answer—"because I shot it. Why do you ask?"

"Sorry, that came out wrong," I apologized. "What I meant was, what kind of detail did you get? I am wondering if you have anything on film that might show if Moira had a small space heater in her booth?"

"A what?" Jeff asked. "You mean one of those little things that plug in? I don't remember seeing anything like that offhand, but it might not have registered with me. Do you want me to go back and look?"

"Would you? That would be great. And if you find anything, can you let me know? At this number?"

"Sure. I don't mind," Jeff said. "It might take a bit. I'm up on the top of the island, shooting some B-roll for one of my other clients, but I'll get to it as soon as I can. Will that work?"

"Thanks. Appreciate it."

I looked at my phone when I ended the call, before I put it away. If I was lucky, Jeff had film of the heater being in the booth of someone who'd said she couldn't remember it. With evidence like that, the pressure might be off Jimmy and redirected toward Moira. The possibility that I might undo some of the damage I had done lifted my spirits.

It was only when I remembered that Stuart had more or less asked me to leave things alone that I felt guilty.

I spent the rest of the day at the store. We were busy, but I still had time to catch up on inventory. The long Victoria Day holiday weekend was ahead, and the first influx of tourists would be arriving. Working with my hands, folding, dusting, rearranging displays, and counting our stock, gave my overfilled mind a rest.

That changed when I looked at my list of incoming stock. A few of the crafters, those who worked at their sewing machines, were late with delivering stock for the Co-op. I wondered if Sheila was right and if some of our sewers had been poached by Terry, and even Louise. I couldn't ask. Whatever the crafters sold through us on consignment was a gift to the concept that the artisan life could be self-sustaining and as a way of sharing our community's traditions. As manager of both the family store and the Co-Op, selling what local people made was my privilege. And for them, supplying that was not an obligation.

Even so, I wanted to know what was going on.

I didn't have to wait long for an answer.

I was at the bottom of the stairs on the main floor, on my way back to the office to get Toby his midday snack, when I heard stiletto-heeled boots on the bowed wooden boards of the store's ancient floor. I didn't need to turn around to know who belonged to those boots. Uncomfortable footwear, the kind that would make standing all day at a craft show torture, had its own distinctive sound. I walked to the front of the store to meet Louise Haggerty.

The visiting designer had tapped her way up to our empty front counter and was pounding the old teacher's bell we'd put there for ironic purposes.

"Well, hello there," I said. "Can I help you?"

"I hope so," she said. "You people are totally stressing me out."

It didn't seem to me that this was an unfair arrangement. You get what you bring to a relationship. "Sorry to hear that," I responded, as a good retailer would. "What seems to be the problem?"

Louise lowered today's bright-pink cat eyeglasses down a nose that was not the one she had been born with. There were rhinestones on the frames of those glasses. I thought that made them look more cheerful than her face.

"Deadlines." She looked hard at me, as if she thought this was a concept local people would not understand. "Deadlines," she repeated. "Do you know what those are?"

I took a moment and a breath. "Oh, I think I do," I said. "Have you ever heard of the lobster season? It's something we have around here; in our zone, the boats have from April 19 to June 20 to do their fishing, that's it. Doesn't matter the weather or the conditions—when it's done, it's done. A year's worth of income."

"Oh, I had no idea." Louise shook her head like an impatient horse at a fence. "I only eat lobster, not catch them. I found out last week they're not born red. I know nothing about fishing. But," she added, recovering, "it sounds like the same concept as Fashion Week."

It was my turn to be confused. I thought of the men I knew standing on the bows chugging out to sea in the rain, rubber boots and waders all the way up to their armpits. Not exactly runway material.

I was wrong about that.

Louise waited for me to agree, and when I didn't, she continued. "The shows," she said. She held up a hand. "Not like that show you just had in that drafty arena. A real show. An event where all the major designers present the new lines for the season. Buyers and manufacturers from all over the world come in. So do the trendspotters, the influencers. The best ideas are picked up and sent to Asia for knockoffs."

I felt insulted. Gasper's Cove wasn't exactly nowhere, whatever this woman thought. We traveled. We went to weddings out of the province, to funerals, to honeymoons, for extra education. And even if we didn't, we had recently gotten almost-reliable-depending-on-the-weather internet in.

"I know what you're talking about," I said, hoping she'd notice how well I'd matched the stripes on my blouse. "I know fashion." This was my opening. "Is that why you're here? Really, I mean. To get local women to sew up samples for your show?" I was proud of myself. This woman would learn that the locals could be pretty sharp. "Is that why our sewers are signing NDAs?"

Louise looked like I had slapped her, and that made me feel bad. It was alright to be smart, but not good to be rude.

"Who told you that?" she asked. "Has someone been talking?"

"You mean your workers? No, of course not. If you tell us to keep a secret, we will." This was only sometimes true, but I was counting on this woman from New York to not know that. "Something I wondered, that's all." I reached for something more plausible to say. "You're not the only one setting people up to do production sewing. I understand Terry is going to do something similar himself."

"That tartan tourist man?" Louise swatted away what might have been an invisible, and maybe Scottish, fly. "He and I aren't in the same business at all. He's interested in the old. I am interested in the Next New Thing. That's where the sales are."

I failed to see how working with old quilts cheated off the beds like in the Bluenose Inn were the Next New Thing, but then again, I knew about making originals, not knocking them off.

"And what's the big new trend going to be?" I asked.

"Wouldn't you like to know?" Louise asked.

I realized I didn't—in fact, I couldn't care less—but I was a shopkeeper and professionally obligated to be courteous.

"Alright then, keep it to yourself." I swept my gaze around the main floor of our store. "What would I know? This time of year, our best sellers are rubber boots. The same kind we've been selling for 80 years."

Louise's head snapped back to me. "Say that again," she said, "the part about your best sellers."

"Rubber boots?" I asked. "The normal kind. Black with orange soles. Same as everyone wears."

Louise looked around, searching the aisles for signs of spies from New York Fashion Week. "I'll tell you what the image is. But if you share any of this with anyone, I'll have to kill you."

I thought this over. Possibly worth the risk.

"In that case, I won't breathe a word, not to a soul. What's the big new idea?"

Louise leaned in. She was wearing a lot of perfume, and not the kind they sold at the drugstore in Drummond.

"The Look of the Season," she paused again, to check the vicinity for undercover fashionistas or maybe ready-to-wear assassins. "No one has ever done it before."

"And it is ...," I asked. Now, I really wanted to know.

"I came up with the concept myself," the designer said, amazed at her brilliance. "And the name too. We're calling it 'The Fisherman's Aesthetic.' Totally original. Nothing like it before."

CHAPTER FOURTEEN

It took me a minute to take in what Louise meant.

"Fisherman's *aesthetic*?" I asked. The two words had nothing in common, nothing at all. I wondered if this woman knew that real fishermen wore green thermal boots with steel toes in them. Wait till the Crafters heard this one, I thought, then remembered this was another secret I had been asked to keep.

Louise leaned in and whispered in my ear.

"Heavy sweaters," the New York designer breathed. "Cables. Ones that look like they have been washed so many times that they are almost felted. Bagged out at the bottom. Holes. Darning. Frayed bottoms. Wide, short pants."

"You mean floods?" I asked. This woman was observant, I gave her that.

Louise shushed me as if I had shared a trademark out loud. "If that's what you call them, yes."

"Rain gear?" I suggested, realizing that on this topic, by birth and location, I was an expert. "Jackets with hoods, sealed seams, and storm flaps? Yellow bib overalls with foot straps? Suspenders?" Mentally, I traveled through aisle six, where we kept workwear. "Work gloves? Yellow leather ones, or the blue ones they wear for lobster? Knee pads? Baseball hats that look like some dog chewed them? Balaclavas? Wool toques?" I thought of the dress code on the wharf across from the store on the other side of Front Street. "Not exactly glamorous or flattering," I suggested.

Louise rapped her toes again on our old boards, sending out some kind of Morse code message of irritation. Briefly, I wondered if her mother had sent her to tap-dancing lessons as a child. There was muscle memory in those feet.

"You don't get it," she said. "It's not about the clothes; it's about the life they evoke. One with a single, clear purpose. Sustainable. Simple. I wouldn't be here if I didn't have to be. I have investors. They want a new collection. They want something unapologetic, stoic, but at the same time, easy." Louise's chin was out, straining the tendons in her neck. "They want me to give them *laid-back*. Do you know how much pressure that is?"

I didn't. But then again, my mind was stuck on the image of yellow waders walking down the streets of New York. I had another thought. "Okay, but how do the boots-and-rain-jacket look fit in with your recycled quilted jackets?" At least the folks across the wharf would only be copied. They wouldn't have to sign any NDAs about their own lives.

Louise pondered the question and then spoke slowly, pronouncing each word carefully so I could keep up. "Every collection these days must have outerwear, casual wear, and evening wear. If it doesn't, the ready-to-wear market isn't going to buy the ideas."

This made sense, sort of. “Right. So, rain jackets and rubber boots are outerwear, quilted clothes are casual, but what are you going to do for the fancy stuff?” I tried to think of pictures I had seen. Of tall, impossibly thin models, slouching down the runway, sequined dresses slipping off boney, breastless chests. Who in a fishing community like Gasper’s Cove was built like that? And where would we wear a sequined dress? No one I knew even owned one, except Darlene, and probably her mother, and her grandmother, but they were not representative. Local legends weren’t.

For the first time, Louise smiled. “The universe,” she said, “brought me here. I was beginning to despair, but my angels solved all my problems at the craft show.”

“They did?”

“Yes. It’s brilliant. Now, I have both the concept and the supplier.” For once, this woman was enjoying herself. “Wait for it,” she said, like she was pulling out the winning ticket in a 50/50 draw. “Kilts. Full length, with metallic granny-square halter tops.”

This was too much. Louise Haggerty didn’t need to worry about finishing me off if I spilled the beans. Her fashion idea was already killing me.

My conversation with Louise, as top secret as it was, was a welcome break from the tension of recent days. The longer it settled in that Stuart was annoyed with me, the more unsettled I felt. He was the first man in my life who knew who I was. This included parts of me that made him uncomfortable and made me uneasy. About myself, about him, about us.

In the earlier stages of my life, when I had been married to my children's philandering father, I had assumed responsibility for all problems and tried to reshape myself to fit. But I wasn't that person anymore. I wasn't sure if I could do that again, and most of all, I realized I did not want to.

I was who I was now. Back from the city in the small community where I had grown up, now I felt more like the girl I had been when I was young. When a person recaptures that, they can't give it up.

I had to listen to my intuition.

And what was it telling me?

Something Heidi had said in my class. That she wasn't someone who liked loose ends.

Neither did I.

I needed Stuart to understand I hadn't meant his nephew any harm. I wasn't the one who had started the rumors. But I cleaned up my own messes.

That was who I was.

Couldn't Stuart see that?

Maybe I didn't know him as well as I thought.

That disturbing idea followed me home after Toby and I closed the store. As we walked away from the waterfront and up the hill to the house, we dawdled. Toby detoured often off the sidewalk to force his nose under bushes and around lamp posts, to smell the earth finally free of the frost. I felt Stuart with me like a shadow. To distract myself, I stopped to talk to my neighbors, who were bundling broken branches and carefully clearing away collapsed streamers of last year's yellow grass to make room for the bulbs erupting in the flower beds. At the turnoff to our street, my dog and I paused to investigate an old tree surrounded by a five-foot radius of wood chips. We looked up and saw that a pileated woodpecker, the largest species of woodpecker in North America, had cut a shoebox-size burrow high in the trunk for its nest.

This made me feel better, reminded me of myself. We humans are not the only crafters.

It was nearly seven o'clock when Toby and I finally climbed the front steps of our house. We were both hungry. I fed Toby first. I was too tired for anything complicated. Then, I remembered the cooked lobster in the fridge, brought over by a neighbor when the season opened, and early greens from the garden. I pulled the lettuce out of the fridge and laid the bright orange-red cooked lobster on my wooden cutting board.

Like every other Nova Scotian, I had been opening lobster my whole life. I worked fast. First, I twisted the tail off the body, then did the same to the legs. Next, I opened a drawer and took out my kitchen scissors. These I used to cut the body down the middle, so I could pull the two sides apart like the pages of a book, to expose the meat. That done, I used the scissors to slice up the legs and to cut the claws off. I'd use a skewer later to dig out the slick parcels of flesh.

But first, I had to break the claws where the shell of the lobster was thickest. I tossed the scissors into the sink and reached into my second drawer to find the old knife with the heavy bone handle to smash the claws open, just like my father had taught me to do. I tugged the drawer open. I lifted the knife out. It caught on something. I pulled the drawer out farther and revealed a folded sheet of parchment paper.

My hands shook as I laid it on the counter and unfolded it.

There it was.

Again.

A large parchment paper heart.

Words were written on it in slanted, masculine letters.

MIDNIGHT. WHERE WE WERE THE LAST TIME I SAW YOU.

There was no signature, because I didn't need one.

Gilles DeWolf was back.

CHAPTER FIFTEEN

I thought I would never see Gilles again.

I thought he was gone, as a criminal fleeing arrest would be.

But he was back.

He'd been in my house and left a calling card that only I would understand. That only I would know how to read.

For me to meet him at a place only he and I knew.

My intuition had tried to prepare me for this. It had failed.

I tore the parchment paper heart into tiny pieces, so small they could not be reconstructed. I let them fall like snowflakes into the trash bin under the sink until they settled at the bottom, where they couldn't be found. Where I couldn't see them.

As soon as I had done that, I felt faint. Destroying the evidence didn't change who had been here. I pulled out one of the chrome-legged chairs at the Formica-covered table and dropped into it.

I had to think.

But all I had were memories.

I'd met Gilles DeWolf, an RCMP communications officer, a few years before. He'd come to Gasper's Cove from Québec as part of an investigation into forged artwork, among them forgeries of paintings by the famous Nova Scotian folk artist Maud Lewis. He was handsome, charming, and, it turned out, the head of the forgery operation he was investigating. But I didn't know that then. And until I did, Gilles had inserted himself into the community and into my life. He'd been in this kitchen before. He had once cooked me a romantic dinner in this room. The original paper heart then had been used to wrap a veal dish, *veau en papillote*, served with wine and his intentions.

But those intentions had been cut short when Officer Dawn Nolan had figured it all out. But by then, Gilles was already gone, one step ahead of his former colleagues.

But now, for some reason, and at considerable risk, he was back on Canadian soil, here again in Gasper's Cove. And he wanted me to know it.

I felt like I had been hit. But still, somewhere, deep inside the compartment where I kept the things I didn't want to think about, I wasn't surprised. A sense of coming trouble had been building inside me for a while. I had tried to push it down, ignore it.

First, Murray died.

Then, things got complicated with Stuart.

Now this.

The last sign of Gilles in Nova Scotia had been the Peugeot he'd left behind in the parking lot of the ferry to Newfoundland. The Newfoundland Constabulary told the RCMP they suspected he'd then fled to St. Pierre and Miquelon, the French islands only 90 minutes from the

Newfoundland coast. These islands gave him a direct way to enter the European Union from North America without crossing a border. For a Francophone seller of forged art, with capital in euros and customers in Europe, what better place to be?

In another time, American gangsters had felt the same way for different reasons and had stationed themselves in those same islands. I remembered the steel walls in the shed on Nancy's property. The gangsters who had set up local fishermen to take bootlegged booze down to the gangsters of New York.

That another criminal, a much more sophisticated one, had used the same location as a portal to life safe from the law, was of no surprise. But then why had Gilles returned to the one place where we knew what he had done?

Why was he back? Why did he want to see me?

I read another message in that paper heart. It was also a sign to me that Gilles DeWolf believed that he could come and go, in and out of my life, whenever he wanted.

How dare he?

The shock wore off, and when it did, anger moved in. I would not sit around in my home and wait for what that man would do next. I would not waste energy trying to figure him out. I was going to act. Let him know that a paper heart didn't impress me.

Not one bit.

For nearly two hours, I considered calling Stuart, but I didn't. Whatever Gilles was involved in, I didn't want him near Stuart. With one last look at my great-grandmother's brown teapot on my counter, I left Toby on the couch and went out to the car. No one was going to stalk me. No one was going to come into my home uninvited.

Gilles had told me where to find him.

I drove there. Along the dark street, past the houses of my sleeping neighbors, up to the top of the island, past woods where only hunting animals were awake, while I tried to think of what would have brought Gilles back to a place where we knew what he was.

Duck had said that criminals cared more about revenge than money. Was that why Gilles was back? Revenge? But against who?

I would find out soon enough.

I was almost there, at the look-off where Gilles and I had had our last conversation, before he stepped into his French car and vanished.

I kept driving. It was early.

I had time.

Even though there was no one behind me, I flicked on my indicator when I made the turn. Darlene and I used to pick blueberries along this old remnant of logging road when we were kids. It was overgrown now, the muddy ruts faded, but clear enough for me to park about twenty feet in, where no one might see my car from the road.

I'd approach the look-off on foot. If Gilles showed up, I wanted to see him before he could see me. I would take my time and wait.

I found the path, thinly shielded by trees from the road, and started walking. Once a truck passed me, headed off the way I'd come, and I stopped to crouch down to avoid its headlights. A hundred yards ahead, I could see the look-off and its view over the cliffs to the Atlantic. I could make out the shape of it, the swing of gravel off the main road, the inadequate safety barrier of a stone wall, the shed of the old weather station near the bushes.

No one was there. The only sound was the unseen Atlantic crashing on the rocks below.

I kept going until I reached the weather station, a wooden shed built before the days of satellite reports and digital information. If I hid behind it, no one driving in from the main road would know I was there. I pressed my body into the bushes and waited. Above me, a cloud passed over the moon. I touched the winder on my old watch and illuminated the face.

Twenty minutes to midnight.

I settled in to wait.

It didn't take long.

Soon, I heard it. A car coming down the road. Headlights lit up the bushes near me and turned in.

Afraid I might be seen, I moved in closer to the shed. A car door opened and then another.

The cloud moved away from the moon. Out on the water, I saw the jagged reflection of its light on the waves.

Carefully, I moved my head enough so I could see who had parked.

I was not prepared for what I saw.

There, at the far end of the semicircle of parking spots, angled out to the ocean, under a tall light, was a white RCMP cruiser. Even from where I was, I could see the elaborate crest, the crown above a buffalo, "RCMP" to one side of it, "GRC" on the other. *Royal Canadian Mounted Police. Gendarmerie royale du Canada.* One of each.

I stepped out from behind the shed and walked forward to meet them both.

Officer Dawn Nolan of the Drummond and Gasper's Cove detachment, and with her another RCMP officer, but a former one, gone rogue and returned from parts unknown.

The one and only Gilles DeWolf.

CHAPTER SIXTEEN

As I walked out of the darkness, Nolan stepped forward. Under the light, I saw she wore a short-sleeved gray shirt under a padded black vest, "Police" in white letters, blond, curly hair showing under the edges of her patrol hat. As I watched, Nolan tucked in her hair, put her hands on her hips and her fingers in her belt, near her pistol, and her Taser.

Next to her was Gilles. He looked a little heavier, a little older, than when I had seen him last, but he was otherwise unchanged. He wore scrubs like a dentist or a doctor.

Except his were bright orange.

It was clear where Gilles DeWolf had been.

In prison.

But Dawn Nolan had brought him out here, in the dark, high above the ocean, to meet me. If this was some kind of new rehabilitation program, I was not impressed.

Nolan stepped forward.

"Valerie, I didn't think you'd be here, but DeWolf said you would." She looked sideways at Gilles, a few feet away from her, and not in handcuffs, I noticed. "I guess there's something going on between the two of you. Not my business." I stared at her but didn't say anything. Even in the dim light, I saw Dawn Nolan's disapproval. "As you can see, DeWolf is now a temporary resident in our prison system," she continued, "the reasons for that, he will say. My part is to explain the situation to you. There's been an increase in criminal activity in the area, and it seems to be coming from this community. DeWolf wanted to talk to you. I'm here on behalf of the RCMP to inform you that what you hear from him tonight is confidential. Before we can proceed, I need your assurance that you will absolutely abide by that."

How could I say no? "Sure. But what's this about?"

Nolan sighed. I could tell she didn't like any of this. Not one bit. She was by nature and occupation an anti-sneaky kind of woman. Being out here in a gravel parking lot, in the dark, with a criminal and a sewing teacher was not her style.

"DeWolf is involved in an investigation that he believes you can help us with. Are you comfortable with that?"

The wind picked up and swirled around me as if it were as confused as I was. Comfortable? Was she kidding?

"Guess so," I answered.

Gilles took over. "Officer Nolan, if you please, can you wait for me in the car? This won't take long." The tone of his voice made it sound as if he were Nolan's superior officer, something that bothered me, and I'm sure bothered her.

To my amazement, Dawn Nolan just nodded, opened the cruiser door, and sat down in the driver's seat. She watched as Gilles guided me about 30 feet away to sit on a bench next to the stone wall, away from the light.

I stared at the orange scrubs. Polyester twill, easy to maintain, but without pockets, which made sense. A one-size-fits-all approach, which meant it would fit nobody.

"You got arrested," I said. "Big surprise there. And now what? They let you out to cut out paper hearts and leave them in people's kitchens? Or look at the ocean in the dark?" I was mad, and I was tired. My worst combination. "That sounds sensible."

Gilles smiled with his eyes. He was enjoying this. That annoyed me.

"What's all this about? Tell me everything. From the beginning. Before you start with anything about the big secret investigation Nolan talked about."

The smile faded. Gilles shrugged.

"*D'accord.* Where do I start? Business, I think." He leaned in closer to me, and I slid to the other end of the bench. "After I left, it went well, but then it did not. Intelligence became artificial, and when that happened, it removed the art from art forgery. It was tasteless and ugly, but these AI algorithms, or whatever they call it, can reproduce the masters more accurately than any of my people could. After many centuries of perfecting the craft, we were replaced. It is painful to say this, but as a broker between artisan and buyer, I was suddenly redundant. I never felt like a thief or a criminal. I was simply a connoisseur, making the masters more accessible. Do you know," he asked, "they can scan a painting now and a computer, not a human with a soul, but *a computer*, can tell if it is an original or not?!"

"Is that how you were caught?" I asked.

"Caught?" I had offended him. "Please. The mice do not catch the cat. Not unless he is hungry. And I was. I have a lifestyle to maintain, and I didn't want it to decline in retirement. I did an inventory of my skills. I looked at the assets I retained. And I realized I was a unique person in a unique position."

I wondered what those assets might be, apart from his charm. "What are you talking about? Cooking? Snappy repartee?"

"Ha, you're quick yourself," Gilles said. "And that's why you're here." The moonlight caught the new creases in his face. He was one of those men who would be even more attractive as he aged. "I would have thought my gifts were apparent. Not many have my experience," he continued. "I have seen fraud from both sides. I needed postretirement income. I couldn't rejoin the RCMP. I was on their wanted list, after all. But I could use my knowledge of both the illegal and legitimate worlds to my advantage. I like to see myself as a translator, a mediator between the criminal and law enforcement experiences. So, I offered my services to my former colleagues and their US counterparts." He smiled. "There's no point in being modest. They snapped me up." He leaned forward. I didn't know that cologne was allowed in jail. "Plus, I live in a world fueled by rumors. I listen. I have always been able to stay ahead of trouble because I can anticipate it. One thing I heard whispered about was of new smuggling activity starting up around Nova Scotia. That was my opening."

"You came back to get in on it?" This seemed risky to me, but then again, my idea of dangerous living was quilting without a walking foot.

"No, no. I am not a criminal. I am simply one who appreciates the fine arts and wanted to share them more widely. Contraband these days is crude. And I am not speaking only about drugs. Craftsmanship is dead. The most precious commodities these days are not things of beauty but whatever makes the most money. Authenticity is no longer valued."

"Right." Clearly the man's irony detector was as broken as his morals. "I'm still missing the part about why you're back here. Do you know what's going on?"

Gilles looked at me as if I had insulted him. "Not specifically, not yet. But from both my former occupations, I have knowledge of people in the area who have, what can we say ... a predilection for smuggling. If anyone can get them to talk, I can. But of course, to be credible in the criminal community, I must go where the criminals are."

"You mean jail?" I asked.

Gilles looked down at his orange outfit and shook his head. "I know. The clothing is terrible. But"—he sat up on the stone wall with almost military determination—"it is a sacrifice I am most willing to make. For Canada"—he paused to collect my admiration—"and a pardon, a clearing of my past criminal record."

The sea was doing its night shift and cooling down the land. I was cold. It was dark. I wanted to go home. I'd had enough of Gilles DeWolf.

"Good luck to you," I said. "But how do I fit into this scheme?"

"I know you." Gilles lowered his voice. I raised my defenses. "You, Valerie, enjoy the intrigue as much as I do. And we have a job that only you can do."

"I'm not going to prison for you," I said. "I have a dog, he's a rescue, I'm all he has, and that is not my color."

Gilles waved the idea aside. "Look, the Mounties are very competent. I was one, I would know. As are our compatriots internationally and on the American side of the border. Certainly, to have me as their 'inside man' is of significance, but we are missing something in our pursuits."

"What's that?" I asked, looking once more at the orange outfit. "Need alterations?"

"No. What we need are eyes and ears in the community, someone who is in and out of everything that happens. We have one other person working for us undercover, but they do not have your contacts. No one else does. You won't be on your own. Anything you see that might be a bit unusual, you can pass on to this operative."

I stared at the former RCMP officer. How did anyone as close to real trouble as he was get all this gall?

"Are you crazy?" I asked. "Why should I help you? I don't owe you any favors. I'm glad you're in jail. That's the only feeling I have about you. Come up with something better than that. Leave me out of this. Get your secret agent to deal with it."

Gilles raised both his hands, palms up, a gesture of exasperation. "Who do you think asked us to recruit you? He did."

I stood up. I had had enough. More than enough. What a night. I remembered the box of emergency chocolate ice cream in the bottom drawer of the freezer. Fifteen minutes and I could be back at home with a bowl and a spoon.

"Really now? And who would that be? Anyone I know?"

"I think you do," Gilles said. "Smart young man. Name of Jimmy MacNeil."

CHAPTER SEVENTEEN

I sat back down on the rock wall.

"I don't believe you. Jimmy is an electrician, not an undercover cop."

Gilles didn't respond. Instead, he waited for me to finish or run out of energy and indignation. Somewhere down below in the dark surf, a seabird called, mocking me too. I scrambled for some reason for my disbelief. "Hey, you guys had him in the detachment for questioning. How about that? His uncle was with him, that's exactly what he told me." Gilles must have mixed up Jimmy with one of Gasper's Cove's other RCMP informants. Clearly, the lack of intellectual stimulation in prison had eroded the man's brain.

"Ah, the uncle." Even in the moonlight, I caught the eye roll. "Mr. Campbell. Showed up uninvited, wanted to be in the room." Gilles snorted. "We made him wait. Left him in the reception area with the *National Geographics*." He reached out and patted my hand. "We have you to thank," he said. "Your little story about the heating unit plugged in at the craft show. How MacNeil had taken it away. It was meaningless, but excuse enough for us to bring him in, and as it turned out, he was exactly who we needed. For other reasons."

It was too late at night for Gilles's slow on-ramp to the truth. If he had something to say to me, I wanted him to say it so I could go home.

"Make your point, DeWolf," I said, trying to sound tougher and more in control than I was, fooling no one. "Chilly, were you? Needed a heater? And then you decided what the RCMP needed was an undercover electrician?" Even from a distance, I felt Nolan's eyes on me. She knew I was about to find out what was going on.

Gilles decided to give up on the charm, which was a relief to at least one of us, and cleared his throat.

"Do you know what a Gideon board is?"

I hated board games; they interfered with both knitting and conversation. I shook my head.

My ignorance didn't surprise Gilles. "I'll make this as simple as possible. Gideon circuit boards are extremely valuable. They contain semiconductor chips, capable of processing incredible amounts of information in seconds. Apparently, this is critical to the development of that artificial intelligence, AI." I could see that the errant RCMP officer would never forgive this new forgery-retiring technology for being invented. "They are so unique that the United States, where the newest ones are made, has extremely strict export controls on who can get access to them. Some of the technological economies in the East, in particular, would give anything to get their hands on them." He let me absorb the implications.

It didn't take me long. "You mean there is some kind of reverse rum-running going on around here?" I asked. "Except instead of us sending down booze to the US, these board things are being smuggled up here and somehow routed to buyers in Asia?"

Gilles smiled at me, his protégé. "You have it, *ma cherie.* That is, more or less, what is occurring."

"But you don't know it all, do you?" I asked. "Not the important parts, like the how and the who. But why me? And Jimmy?"

"You have always brought me luck," Gilles said. "This is no exception. You see, when we questioned Mr. MacNeil about this silly heater, we probed and found the real reason he had retrieved it. You see, your Jimmy is not without ethics, and for some time he had been doubting his employer and this appliance-refurbishing scheme. After all, as he said himself, why would anyone go to the trouble of sending returned merchandise and replacement parts all the way here to get the work done? To, what do those around here call it, 'Last Gasp'? It makes no sense, unless it is a way of getting small electronic components across the US/Canadian border. These priceless circuit boards, the latest ones, are like layers of waffles, no more than twelve inches square. For transport, we suspect they are interfiled with the ordinary boards. Not many border or customs agents, inspecting trucks en route to nowhere, could tell the difference between a Gideon board and other electronic components."

I couldn't help myself. "Pretty clever," I admitted." My mind ran ahead. "And Jimmy found some of the special boards? Is that it? Is that why you pulled him in?"

"Not precisely," Gilles admitted. "We are fairly certain that the Gideon boards are removed somewhere in this process. The boards Mr. MacNeil was given to do replacements were cheap and barely effective. That's what had him worried, why he wanted to check the unit. His only concern at that point was quality, not contraband. This is what he explained to us when we had our conversation. But I do not believe in accidents. I believe in fate." Gilles made a move to take my hands, but I folded them under my arms. "This Jimmy, he is a reliable person, the kind who wants to do the right thing. He is also as close to the delivery side of this operation as we will find. We have asked him to, discreetly, see if he can ascertain when and how the Gideon boards are being picked up and removed from the shipment. And, of course, by whom."

This made some sense to me. It was obvious that it might take a criminal mind to catch a criminal, but just as obvious that it took a straight arrow to do the dangerous work.

The sea bird called again, insistent.

Imports, exports. Murray Nunn was some kind of economic development facilitator. That's what Darlene told me. He was at the craft show, looking for 'new opportunities.' It all made sense now. "Murray was some kind of Mr. Big, am I right? Your buddies in jail probably tipped you off."

"Clever girl, but Nunn was more the man in the middle than the one on top. And possibly the only one who liked to talk."

I knew where this was going. "Holy moly. Someone did fool around with Murray's pacemaker, didn't they? The gang killed him." We'd heard the stories about rum-running gangsters from our grandparents. "It was a hit."

Gilles didn't say I was wrong.

And now Jimmy was being sent into the middle of it all.

"Sounds dangerous for Jimmy," I said. "Hope he's careful."

"He will be. He understands," Gilles said. "The sooner we get to the bottom of this, the sooner it will be over, and he will no longer be involved."

I understood then why Gilles was so good at both sides of his career. He could sense a weak spot and go right to it. He knew mine: I wanted Stuart's nephew safe.

"What do you want me to do? Now's the time to tell me." Toby wasn't used to being alone at night. He would be worried.

Gilles laughed. "When we made our proposal for cooperation to Mr. MacNeil, he said that he wasn't sure if he was cut out to spy on anyone, that this sounded more like your kind of work. He's heard the stories about things you have done in the past. He was right, of course. There are two parts to this operation. One is importing the boards from the US. It makes sense for them to be shipped to the Far East from the middle of nowhere, so much less likely than, say, if they tried to send them directly from the Port of San Francisco. Sophisticated minds behind this. The thing is, even if we understood how the illegal boards are getting in and who is collecting them, we would have solved only half of the puzzle. We would still need to know how, once the boards are here in this most inconsequential place, they are leaving this continent and going to the end customer."

There was frustration and hurt ego in Gilles's voice. He was smart enough to have been a high-ranking RCMP officer and to have been a high-living thief. He was offended that despite both achievements, he still couldn't figure out how a crime of this scale was being executed in Gasper's Cove.

"This is back to how no one but a small-town woman knows better what is happening in a small town? You want me to keep a look-out for anything from here being shipped overseas, disguised as something else? That has to be part of it, am I right?" I asked. "This isn't a 'go down to the Canada Post, put a few semiconductor chip boards in a padded envelope, and fill out a customs declaration' sort of situation, is it?"

"*Non*," Gilles said. "As I explained to my former superiors, there is only one person who can make these inquiries."

This didn't sound entirely like a compliment. "And why is that?" I asked.

"You can't help yourself. You are curious," Gilles said. The light was good enough for me to catch the wink. "If it is your business or not. People are used to this from you—involving yourself. They won't think anything of it."

I started to object, but Gilles was right. I had to admit that.

I moved on to the logistics. A place where we were both more comfortable. "If I find anything out, why do I take it to Jimmy and not to you?"

"Think about it," Gilles said. "The fewer discernible routes for information back to me in prison, or to the RCMP, the better. Jimmy is the only one who can be seen with the Mounties. It will be interpreted as if he is still under investigation."

"You think people will believe that?"

"Of course they will. Why wouldn't MacNeil talk to the RCMP? After all, the man already has a poor reputation. Thanks to you."

CHAPTER EIGHTEEN

When I finally got home, after 2:00 a.m., I was too wound up and tired to sleep. I didn't even try. Instead, I walked the narrow hallway of my 1950s bungalow and tried to understand what had happened. Usually, the house at night gave me answers. It was as if, when the rest of us were quiet, it had a chance to speak. But tonight, it was silent, waiting with me for answers, but more confident than I was that they would come.

Nolan had been curt when I said goodbye in the look-off parking lot. It was clear she didn't endorse any operation that pulled in civilians. I got the impression that she would be more than happy to put Gilles DeWolf back behind bars.

However, the former and disgraced RCMP officer was right about one thing: The sooner this was over and whoever had murdered Murray was carted away, the sooner Jimmy would get his life back and my relationship with Stuart would settle down into its comfortable place.

I didn't let myself consider that this might not happen.

So, I paced up and down the hall, past all the framed family pictures that had come with the house—come with my past. There was Darlene and me on our bikes, our mothers at their weddings, and portraits of the dogs, my grandfather's water spaniel fresh from the ocean, the terrier that would let anyone into the house but nipped at their ankles if they tried to leave. Generations of good dogs. Some of those pictures were black and white, from a time when the mind filled in the colors. Others, those on the wall facing the window, had faded into pastels, reminding me of how many years ago it had been since we had all looked that young. I wanted those simple days back. That would not happen.

Plus, the present was keeping me busy. I remembered how Gilles had described the fancy AI-enabling boards. He used the word *waffles*, wafers, layers of materials. The way I visualized that made me think of top, backing, and batting.

A quilt.

And who did *that* make me think of?

Louise Haggerty.

She was new to town and involved in exports. She knew Murray. And the first time I met her, at the bottom of the stairwell in the arena, she had made it clear she didn't like him, and the why mattered. Did she have a reason to kill the consultant?

Murray had a bad heart and a pacemaker. He had been shocked to death by someone who knew his health history and knew him well enough to get close enough to him to cause harm.

He was a stranger to town. The only people who knew him well were his clients.

Again, Louise Haggerty.

I walked into the kitchen and snapped open a tin of oatcakes to help me think. I went over to the sink and ate two, looking out into the dark backyard, letting the crumbs fall. I turned on the tap to wash them down the drain and looked at the bright-pink knitted dishcloth that had come from the Co-op. I knew why some of my crafters were working more slowly than usual: A few, I suspected, were doing production work for the refashioning designer.

Who had made them sign confidentiality agreements, NDAs.

This explained why no one had shared with me that they were doing this for her, but it still left me wondering why those agreements were even necessary.

I tried to remember what she had told me about her business. Something about samples for New York Fashion Week, about trends, about silly ideas like the 'Fisherman's Aesthetic.' Why was The Next Big Thing a secret? Who would care?

The competition.

It came to me, right there in my kitchen, a damp knitted dishcloth in my hand. Samples made here by local women with reclaimed quilts would be sent first to the New York runways and then to overseas factories to be copied and mass-produced.

Fast fashion inspired by a slow place.

Louise Haggerty was not here to create originals, whatever she said.

Her real business, the real money, was in knockoffs. For exporting. To parts of the world where these Gideon boards were like rum during Prohibition.

Contraband hidden in layers of deceit. After all, what better place to hide anything delicate, like a circuit board, than in between layers of batting? A lightweight component, just a foot square, could be slipped inside a quilted coat, jacket, or tote.

Were the sewers from Gasper's Cove making clothing, or packaging?

Or both?

No wonder Louise had made them sign NDAs.

Suddenly, an early-morning crow called out to me from a tree in the yard. It was the approval of an outlaw telling me I had figured it out.

But I needed proof.

NDA or not, I had to find sewers who would talk.

I knew where I could find them.

I waited until the students had installed the twin needles in their machines and were well into hemming before I went fishing.

"Apart from everything else that went on at the show, there was some lovely work." I threw this out to the class to see who would take the bait. I was in my teacher's chair at the front of the room, doing serious work with a seam ripper on a student's ribbing neckline that had the joining seam at the center front rather than the back. "Particularly those quilted jackets," I said. "Who would have thought?"

"An operator, obviously," Nancy mumbled. Her mouth was full of straight pins. "It's a crime to cut up an heirloom."

I handed over the now-neckline-less T-shirt back to my student, who thanked me before scurrying back to her machine. She was an excellent quilter, but knits made her nervous. It was her fourth time taking this beginner's class.

Nancy moved on. She'd used her old Singer again that night to push the other women away from the space next to Heidi. Now, she offered the young mayor's assistant a cranberry muffin she'd brought from home.

"It's so nice to have something in the family passed down," she confided to Heidi. "Trousseaux, wedding dresses, christening gowns ... " She paused to give the younger woman a chance to add to the list. When she didn't, Nancy switched to a related inquiry. "Your last name is Wallace? Like William Wallace, the hero." She eyed Heidi with the unease of a Noah who had found an unpaired creature in his ark.

Heidi put down her scissors, welcoming the detour from matrimony to genealogy. "I guess so. The family came from Ayrshire. When I was at the show, I was over at Terry's booth. I bought my dad a scarf for Christmas. I told Terry I was learning to sew. He was very interested, even asked if I wanted to make things for him. I guess he's having trouble finding people."

I intervened. "That's right," I said. "I've heard that any of the women who do that kind of sewing are working for Ms. Haggerty. Am I right?"

The friend of the ribbing-challenged quilter lifted her hand. "Yes," she said cautiously, but honoring the Gasper's Cove rule that no one should stay silent if, in any way, they could contribute. "There's a few of us. Good money, and the patterns aren't hard. Front, back, sleeves, binding. Not really supposed to say more than that."

"Oh, I understand," I said, "garments for New York." I wanted to imply I knew more than I did. "That's all you have to do?" I asked. "What about, say, zip-out linings? Or pockets? Really big pockets? Detachable hoods?"

The student attempting to re-pin her ribbing looked up. "Nothing too complicated, no zippers or buttonholes—she likes it simple to make. It's all about the old materials. Mind you, sometimes those get some new fabric worked in ... " Her friend poked her in the side, and she stopped to assess me. "These are detailed questions. Why? Are you interested in taking on some extra work?"

Ha, I thought to myself, that will be the day. For the room, I smoothed my ulterior motive from my face. "I might," I said. Lying was easier than I'd thought. "I might be interested. Do you think you could set something up?"

"Sure, I'll have a word." My sewer took out the pins. She'd done it again. The binding seam was back at the center front. "It's easier than this, that's for sure. Even though, like you said, she likes a lot of pockets."

CHAPTER NINETEEN

I'd hoped my student would pass on my apparent interest in piecework to Louise, but even so, I was surprised when she called the next afternoon. I was in my office, giving Toby his lunch, when the phone on my desk, still on silent from the night before, jumped.

"I understand you teach sewing classes and might be interested in some contract work," the designer/smuggler stated as if it were a fact. No "hello." No "how are you?" "I only have two sewers right now, and their work is a little shaky."

Tell me about it, I thought. I'd seen those ribbing necklines. Most quilters I knew didn't enjoy sewing garments. Beds are easier to fit than bodies.

"I'm thinking about it," I said. I had been thinking about a lot of things, including the reasons why this woman might have killed her export agent at a craft show. "But I need more details." This was true. When I took all this to the RCMP, they would want details, not theories. I knew this from all the times I'd gone to them without any of that.

"Excellent," Louise said. I wasn't sure if the tone of her voice was that she couldn't believe how lucky she was to reach me or that she didn't believe any of this at all. "How about we meet?" she suggested. "Somewhere quiet. Out of the way."

She had to be kidding. That was the last thing I would do.

"Love to," I said, one liar to another. "Working today. How about you come to the store? We can talk in my office." Not far from where Duck and Jimmy, still working on our rewiring, would be, just outside the door.

"I guess so." There was reluctance in the woman's voice. This wasn't her first choice for a meeting place, but it was mine. "Say, after 5:00?"

"Perfect." I'd need that time to get ready. "See you then."

After Louise hung up, I went out into the store to find Jimmy. He was near the back door, not far from the rakes.

"A word?" I whispered from between the sharp tines of our turning-over-the-soil display. "Meet me in my office."

I was behind my desk when Jimmy joined me. He stood because Toby had taken possession of my ancient, upholstered visitor's chair. Toby was there because part one of my plan to confront Louise, the smuggler and murderer, as safely as possible was to have a dog in the room. Part two was to have a secret-agent junior electrician listening outside the door.

"Valerie?"

Jimmy was such a nice-looking young man; maybe Nancy *should* set him up with Heidi. When all this was over.

"Jimmy," I answered.

The conversation stalled.

"I know," I said to move things along.

"You know?"

"Yes, I do."

Silence.

"RCMP," I added. This was the big card, so I played it. "Me too. We're working together."

"I know that," Jimmy said. It was a start. We had established that we were two people who knew things. "Officer Nolan told me," he added, nonstop talker that he was. "Now what?"

It was apparent that Jimmy and I had only a vague idea of what our assignment was. I suspected he'd been told, as I had, to keep his eyes and ears open. As if anyone living was not already doing that.

Our little team needed leadership. "I think I know who did it—who shocked Murray to death, smuggled these boards, all of it."

Jimmy's eyes went wide. He had his uncle's beautiful wasted-on-a-man eyelashes. "You do?"

"I do. Only got to tie up the loose ends," I said. "Proof, things like that. Maybe a confession."

Jimmy still hadn't blinked.

"Who is it?" Toby moved over and made enough room for the young electrician to perch on the edge of the chair. Jimmy and Toby waited, alert. For the first time in my life, I understood the expression "edge of your seat." I gave myself a moment to enjoy it.

"Haggerty. The designer. Murray was in her booth. She's got a local workforce making quilted jackets with AI hidden in the batting. Kind of like smugglers putting rum behind metal walls."

I searched for excitement, maybe some admiration, in Jimmy's face. I couldn't see it.

"That woman? The one who sells recycled clothes or whatever? Are you sure?" I could see that Jimmy had put together his own list of suspects, and Louise's name was not on it. "Where's the evidence?"

"It's coming. At five o'clock. Louise is going to meet me here in the office. I'd like you to hang around tonight, but lie low, in aisle five or something." Mops and brooms. Good coverage. "In case I need backup."

The alert was gone, replaced by the kind of tolerance a sharp young man might feel for an older woman who had lost her edge.

"Alright, I can do that," he said. "Got a few things to finish up." He stroked Toby's head and stood up. "I'm not even going to ask you where you got this idea, but if that designer lady is behind all of this, what do you think is going to happen? You'll ask her if she's a killer and a crook, and she'll just say yes or no?"

I ignored the question. "Just make sure you stay in the vicinity," I instructed. "Don't worry about that part. I have a plan."

Jimmy shrugged and walked through the door and back into the store.

"Good to know."

The truth was, I didn't have a plan. I had an *idea*, but I had realized that was not the same as a plan. However, it was too late to do anything about that.

Instead, I pulled the tin of gingersnaps I had brought from home out of my purse, got ready to make tea, and waited.

Jimmy knocked on the door.

"Someone to see you," he called, as if he had no idea why a visiting fashion designer from New York wanted to see the manager of a general store off the shore of Nova Scotia, right after closing time.

"Come in," I said, nudging Toby out of the worn visitor's chair with one hand and plugging in the kettle with the other.

Louise took one step into my office and paused as if she wanted to take two steps back out.

I appreciated that to the uninitiated, the office might be a disappointment. Situated in the center of the store, closer to the stock-receiving end at the back than to the customer-greeting end out front, the office was not much bigger than my kitchen at home, but windowless. The gloom was not helped by the navy paint that had been applied to the walls sometime back in the 1970s, when that had seemed like a good idea. The oak desk, installed half a century ago, had grown roots into the floor, with a swivel chair behind it, also oak, but not a match, that squeaked when it was swiveled, so no one ever did that. Hard against the outer wall was a bank of three filing cabinets, label-less and, because that's how Rankins did it, with all the folders inside laid down flat, as if they were resting, since vertical alphabetization seemed unnecessary, maybe even pretentious, in a family business where the secrets and records were orally maintained. Inside some of those folders were invoices and receipts from as far back as the Depression, documenting accounts that were run up, never paid, and let go without a word, but kept among us as a record of those hard years, as a reminder of a community that had survived.

Only the wall opposite showed any adaptation to modernity. Along it, mismatched kitchen cupboards had been lined up next to a battered and rust-spotted bar fridge, and a countertop, singed black at one end, so likely salvaged from some fire, laid over it all. Here, because store managing could be a long and hungry business, was a small microwave, a foil-lined toaster oven, and, of course, a kettle.

"Good to see you," I said as I did to every single person I met, murderers no exception. "I was just making tea. Come in and sit down." I pushed Toby back out of his chair, because it was for visitors and we had one. Insulted, he climbed his way into the foot space under the desk, back to us; sighed; put his head on his paws, ears up; and pretended to sleep.

Louise walked over to the chair, assessed its patina of golden retriever hair, looked at her black pants, and said, "I'll think I'll stand."

To be hospitable, I wheeled the protesting managerial swivel chair out from behind the desk.

"Here, you have this chair. I'll sit in that one." I turned on the kettle and poured the gingersnaps onto a plate and put it on the desk. Toby lifted his head and sniffed.

Louise and I both waited until the tea was made before we got to the reason for her visit.

"I understand you might be interested in doing some sewing for me," she said. "I won't ask about your qualifications. You do know it's piecework, don't you? Not a lot of room to be creative."

"I understand that. But I thought it would be a change." I was making this up as I went along. "The idea of making samples for a New York show is exciting. Fisherman's style, recycling quilts as clothes ... I've sewn all my life, but you're the creative one." I took a sip of my tea and coughed. "If you don't mind me asking, how did you get into this?" I was proud of myself. This was a clever way to start. I hoped that if I could get her talking about her life, Louise would reveal what made her detour into major crime.

"I used to sew too," she said. It was a less dramatic answer to my question than I had hoped. "I loved it. I did textile arts in college. I was a poor student, no money for fabric, so I shopped at thrift stores, cut up garments, and remade them. I used quilts because they're large pieces of fabric, already insulated and lined. Perfect for jackets and coats. I started selling them at shows, like the one you had here, and then one day, out of the blue, I was contacted by Bennett Crawford's personal assistant. *The* Bennett Crawford." Louise stopped to let me say, "Wow," which I would have if I had known who this Crawford person was. Which I did not.

"That sounds nice," I said. "Keep going."

Louise picked up a cookie and talked to it. "Bennett's a genius. He can look at ten trends and immediately know which ones will sell to the mass market. He's a legend in the industry. There isn't a garment manufacturer on this planet who would miss any of his shows." She took a nibble of the gingersnap and raised her eyebrows at me. "These are good."

"Thank you," I said. "Family recipe. So, what did Mr. Crawford want?"

"To work with me." Louise was abrupt. The glamour of the association had worn off. "He was onto the sustainable-fashion trend before anyone else, and he wanted me to help launch a new collection. I know that you've refurbished clothing around here for generations, but if you're in New York, it's new, believe me. At first, Bennett just had me sew pieces for him. I went around to shows and collected vintage quilts, like I am doing here. It was important to the brand that we could say everything was authentic. You've got to remember, this was the man who saw grunge coming and only worked with worn-out flannel shirts. Same principle."

I got up and poured myself another tea. This was leading up to whatever had put the bitterness in Louise's voice.

"Sounds like a lot of stress," I suggested.

A look of gratitude sparked and then fizzled on Louise's face. "Exactly. It was hard to keep up. I cut corners. When I couldn't find what I needed, I'd work in some new fabric with the vintage. Bennett found out. He said I had violated the brand, but we were in too deep. There were investors. If he fired me, there would be questions. He gave me one last chance to do something he could sell as the real deal. If I couldn't deliver, I'd be gone. Back to being a nobody." Her laugh was genuine now. "A fraud, working for a fake, selling the real. I know."

It was time to recap. Louise had admitted dishonesty. This was going in the right direction.

"And you came here for a supply of old quilts, looked around, and came up with the idea for this fisherman's look?"

"Yes. Bennett loved it. The buyers will too. What you see on the runway this year will be in Walmart next year. That's how it works."

I picked up the office teapot. "More tea?" Louise nodded, and I poured. "But why Gasper's Cove? And why did you need to be connected to someone like Murray if you already had a boss?" *And, more to the point, why did you want to disconnect him?* I thought.

Louise raised her hands. Money had made her surrender. "You've got to understand, the industry depends on a customer buying, again and again, year after year, whether they need the clothes or not. New is everything. The only thing. The race to find it is ruthless. There were a few subclauses in Bennett's conditions. The first was that wherever we got our materials or ideas, our source had to be someplace so out of the way that none of our competitors would even have heard of it."

She had just described Gasper's Cove. "Alright. But Murray?" I persisted. I thought of the man at the back of a craft show booth, of the flying ducks on his socks going nowhere, of his spotted damp hand with the medical alert bracelet, disguised as jewelry, but still documenting his vulnerability.

"Chance," Louise said, her eyes unfocused as she looked over my shoulder to the past, unsure if she liked the memory or not. "Funny how it happened. I was on my way to an event in Manhattan. When I walked through the lobby, I saw a sign, 'Nova Scotia/US Trade.' You folks had sent down an export delegation, about seafood, mostly. And outside the conference, milling around, was Murray. He was a kind of bottom-feeder looking for minnows like me. He was friendly, and we got to talking. I told him about my situation. I was desperate. He listened. He said he would help me out, hook me up with a craft show in middle-of-nowhere Nova Scotia. That got my attention—that, and what he said next."

"Which was?"

"That the only way to ever be secure was to work for myself, to get away from Bennett and his expectations. I agreed, but I asked how? Without any capital? And Murray told me not to worry. For a retainer, he would guarantee he'd find me money to go out on my own. Something about grant money, municipal support."

"How did that turn out?" I asked. "From your point of view?" I already knew how it had turned out for Murray.

"Terrible," Louise snorted. "He told me what I wanted to hear, so I bought it. Then, that man turned around and used everything I had told him to blackmail me."

I wondered if Jimmy was outside, his ear pressed to the door like mine would have been if I were him. This was it. Why Murray had died. I realized then how foolish I had been. Toby snored under the desk, oblivious. This woman was dangerous. And what did I have to defend myself? A teapot?

"Blackmail?" I choked over the words. From where I sat, my back was to the door; I was trapped.

Louise calmly reached over to the plate on the desk and picked up two gingersnaps. She bit into one and put the other on her saucer. Despite my growing panic, I admired her. This was a woman who understood how to do a confession.

"Blackmail. Remember those competitors? Murray threatened to tell them about this place. This island. The source of my ideas, of our authenticity. Do you know what would have happened next?"

I struggled for an answer, to imagine this woman's world, borrowed supplies and fashion. "Next? That all the old quilts would disappear from every bed in Gasper's Cove? That the store would have a run on rubber boots? Yellow rubberized overalls would be put on back order? Everyone in New York would already dress like fishermen even before the show?" I knew I was babbling, and I didn't care.

Louise snapped the gingersnap in two. At the sound, Toby raised his head. "Exactly," she said. "I couldn't let that happen."

I didn't need to hear, or stay for, anything else. I had my confession. I couldn't risk anything else.

"Toby," I said. "Come here. Treat." On shaky legs, I stood up and backed toward the door, slowly, carefully. "Jimmy," I called out, "you better get in here. Quick."

"Jimmy?" Louise started to talk rapidly, words running together as if she had to tell it all to me before an outsider arrived. "You've got to understand. I didn't want to bring them in, but I couldn't deal with it anymore. Do you believe me? I had no other choice." The teacup in Louise's hand rattled on its mismatched saucer. I realized then that she was as frightened in her own way, and for different reasons, as I was.

"Oh, I think you had lots of choices." The words were out before my mind caught up. "You just made a bad one."

CHAPTER TWENTY

For a second, we were both still, listening. Now that I had called for him, I expected Jimmy to come charging into the office, bringing the cavalry with him—Duck, Shadow, and maybe my aunt Colleen from the front counter. I braced myself for the old doorknob to hit the wall, for Jimmy to arrive, maybe armed with an aisle-five broom to protect me from Murray's killer, or at least someone who had orchestrated his death.

Instead, Jimmy sauntered in, prying up the plastic lid from his Tim Hortons coffee. I had asked him to be on standby while I snapped the trap shut on a well-dressed criminal. Instead, he'd gone out for coffee.

I was disappointed.

"Hey, ladies, how's it going?" he asked, taking a sip from the paper cup.

"How's it going?" I responded. I wanted to get this moment on the record and witnessed. "Louise here was about to tell me about her sideline, high-tech smuggling, and what she does to anyone who stands in her way." It felt good to release my fear into words, as if that would make me safe. Louise's mouth fell open. I didn't expect she thought anyone would figure her out. There was only one detail left to confirm.

I looked at her hard.

"Did you do it yourself?" I asked. "It wasn't the heater at all, was it? My bet's on the clothes steamer. Upright. On wheels. Water, a great conductor." I could see it. Slide the steamer over, zap Murray. Slide it back. I had another thought. "Or was it whoever you called in who shocked him? Am I right?"

There was silence. The look on Louise's face was wary. That was to be expected. But then her mouth shifted to a patronizing smile. This was unexpected.

"Look, I know the fashion scene has its bad actors. You could call it a gang. But I'm not in on it. That's the point. I'm an outsider. And high-tech? You mean the Smart Steamer? Digital? Senses the fiber and self-adjusts? No one irons anymore, do they?"

Not iron? I felt myself steam up. What a low thing to say to a fellow sewer, particularly one in a crisis. I began to mentally compose a well-pressed response.

Jimmy caught my eye and cleared his throat. "Maybe you've said enough, Valerie," he cautioned.

This offended me. I thought Jimmy and I were on the same undercover team. Didn't he know how dangerous this woman was? Outraged, I turned my back on them both. I took a dried liver treat out of the jar. I handed it to Toby and leaned back against the counter. I wasn't giving up.

"Who did you call for help, Louise? You never said. And what did you do to Murray?"

"Murray? What on earth are you talking about?" Louise did a good impression of indignant. But I saw through it. "I did nothing to that man but report him."

That stopped me.

"Report?" I asked. Beside me, Jimmy shifted on his feet.

"Yes, I followed your example," she said, now composed enough to pick up another gingersnap. "I watched you at the show when you went down to talk to that Mountie. So determined. It made me realize I had to stop being intimidated by these pretend business guys. That day, when I saw all those booths, it hit me. You people are tougher than all the Murrays and Bennetts in the world put together. I thought to myself, if they can make a go of it here, of all places, why can't I do the same where it matters? So, I stood up for myself. When I heard that Murray had died, that was it. I went to the RCMP building and talked to Officer Nolan. I explained that he had been blackmailing me. If Murray had enemies, he had made them himself."

"Nolan? That's who you went to for help? Not the rest of your gang?" I needed a tea; my throat felt dry.

"Who else did you think I meant when I said I had no choice but to involve them?" Louise looked confused. "I talked to the Mounties. I had to."

The only sound in the office was Toby crunching his treat.

Jimmy broke the silence. He shrugged at Louise, almost in apology. "A misunderstanding," he said, bending down to rub Toby's ears. "Not much happens in Gasper's Cove. I guess when it does some of us get ... flustered."

Flustered? I stared at Jimmy. Who did he think I was? Some senior in a tizzy? All worked up about nothing?

And then, as if a page had been turned, Louise retreated into sympathy to deflect my accusation. As if acting as if nothing had happened meant nothing had.

"Maybe you need some air, Valerie. You look a little warm. My mom was the same at your age. It's not easy ... " She glanced over at Jimmy and spoke to him. "We'll forget about this."

Louise reached over and patted my hand as if I were another Toby. "Maybe we can talk about the sewing another time. But if you're looking to make a little extra, Terry Kirkpatrick's getting something set up. Maybe he can use you." She looked around the office, her gaze lingering on the burned end of the countertop and the dog hair-covered chair. "I can see you might need it."

After Louise left, Jimmy broke the silence first.

"What were you talking about?" he asked. "A clothes steamer? Where did that come from?"

"A shed. With metal walls," I started.

"Stop, just stop." Jimmy held up his hand and looked down at the floor. "Good thing that woman feels sorry for you. What would Nolan say, or Wade? This was not what we were supposed to do."

"Eyes and ears. I know. I get it," I said. "Loose lips sink ships."

"And you sure sunk that one." Jimmy shook his head. "I'm off. Knit night at Seaview Manor. Elite. By invitation only. I made the cut." He pulled a paper out of his pocket. "Before I forget. While you were in here having your finest hour, I answered the store phone. Your cell must have been on mute. Catherine called from the Inn. She said to tell you she found something for you at the library. Why don't you call her and forget about all of this? Maybe lie low for a bit?"

I gave Jimmy my best sweet, ready-to-be-a-blue-haired-lady smile and tried, with effort, to look as passive as I could. I held the look until the office door closed behind him. Shaky with diverted adrenaline, indignant that no one had taken me seriously, I called the Bluenose Inn.

"Catherine. Sorry, I was in a meeting." Is that what it had been? "But I got the message. What did you find out?"

"Which century do you want me to start in?"

This conspiracy was deeper than I thought. Now, I was getting somewhere. "Whichever you think is relevant," I said, then regretted it. Catherine had started her library career in cataloguing before she went into reference. In her mind, there was no such thing as insufficient detail.

"How about AD 832? The battle of Athelstaneford ... do you want me to spell that out so you can write it down?" she asked.

"I'm good. Is this about the saltire?" I had asked for information about the name of the company buying up orphan land on the coast around the island. I should have been more specific about the time frame.

I had offended my research assistant.

"Of course it is," Catherine assured me. "This is about the birth of an icon. The battle was between an outnumbered King Angus of Scotland and the Angles and Saxons from the south. King Angus prayed for help, and it came just when he needed it: The clouds formed a giant cross in the blue sky. Scared the enemy away because everyone knew it had come from St. Andrew, who had been martyred on a diagonal cross."

"I didn't know any of that," I said. "Pretty dramatic. And that's why we have the cross on the Nova Scotia flag?"

"Yes, and on Scotland's, which, by the way, is the oldest flag in Europe. The saltire is on many clan crests. I can send you a list."

"Interesting, but how does this tell us anything about an investment company, or who is behind it?"

"Obvious," Catherine said. "Whoever is involved must be someone local, or Scottish, and definitely someone with a strong sense of history."

"Go on. Any clues about the company itself?"

Catherine was ready for me. "There are layers," she said. "Many layers. Saltire Investments is owned by a trust, that is itself owned by another trust."

"A trust?"

"They are entities that hold investments on behalf of other persons or agencies."

"Why do that?"

"To create arm's-length distance between management and the source of the financing." Catherine was in her element. "Often, they are set up by people with their own regulatory responsibilities—politicians, public servants, for example—or sometimes when an estate is being managed."

I had no idea what Catherine was talking about. None. I picked up a treat to feed Toby and nearly ate it myself by mistake. I felt unsteady and sat down in the creaking manager's chair Louise had vacated. "But who set it up?"

"Not sure. But I filed a Freedom of Information and Protection of Privacy request with the government. That might tell us."

"Great," I said. "How long will that take?"

"Only six to eight months."

"Oh." At this stage, I didn't need a dead end. Not any more than Murray had. I had learned from Louise that Murray was blackmailing her. What else was he doing? His murder and Saltire Investments had to be connected, but I didn't know how. Murray had been a questionable character, and a blackmailer, but he deserved justice, like we all did. "I really appreciate what you've done, but I was hoping I might find out something sooner."

"Don't underestimate me." The ex-librarian sounded like she had experienced that often enough. "What I do have for you is information on the boats moored opposite the parcels of land Saltire owns. The boats are not there long. Most of them come in during the evening and go in the early morning. But there is documentation."

Toby jumped up and pulled his leash off the edge of my desk. I mouthed "in a minute" to him. The big dog sighed and lay down. "And this intelligence is from who?" I asked.

Catherine wasn't going to tell me until I savored her process.

"The first step was to question the premise," she said. "Number-one rule of effective research. You wanted to know about a company buying up scraps of coastal land. Naturally, you and I"—I could tell she meant me, the premise assumer, and not herself, the analytical thinker—"focused on the land. But think about it. The coast. Water. This property is useless, you said so yourself. Rocky, nowhere to build.

The ocean offshore near these places isn't even part of the fishery. Riptides, not good for beaches. But who loves places like that? And who goes there very early in the morning? Takes pictures? Posts videos?"

I knew. I had a couple of boys who did exactly that when they were home. "Surfers?" I asked.

"You better believe it. I've spent hours on social media. Good swell, locations labeled. But the shots caught boats in the background, on the edges. Near the properties on the list that Saltire owns. Cape Islanders, lobster boats, in areas where they can't fish."

"That makes no sense. Why would they moor there?"

"No idea," Catherine said, "not if they want to fish lobster, but maybe they are up to something else." A doorbell rang in the background. "Look, I've got to go. I'll text you a link to the history. Let me know if you need any other information."

"Thanks."

Catherine hung up, and then my phone pinged with her message. I sat down on my dog fur-covered visitor's chair and clicked the link. There it was, everything she had told me, including a list of flags, such as Nova Scotia's, and clan crests that incorporated the saltire. Many of the family names were familiar. Some were not. One stood out.

A diagonal cross, a hand with a dagger, dripping blood, and a motto.

I make sure.

Clan Kirkpatrick.

CHAPTER TWENTY-ONE

On the long walk up the hill from the store to home, I tried to reframe my suspicions. It was a good thing that the neighbors who smiled and waved as Toby and I passed had no idea what was on my mind.

Crime and murder.

I had been proud of myself for coming up with the idea of circuit boards smuggled in the pockets of quilted coats. It made sense. Cotton batting would have worked well. It was denser than polyester and therefore would be less obvious. Crazy-quilted jackets and coats, sewn with fancy and thicker fabrics, such as velvet or brocade, could easily obscure the feel of a slim circuit board layered behind them.

It was all so smart.

And all so wrong.

I'd tried too hard. The answer to everything lay with someone and something closer to home.

Terry Kirkpatrick had revealed himself and his dishonest hand when he had used the cross on his family crest to name his investment trust. It also wouldn't surprise me if a man so obsessed with history and tradition had taken pleasure in collecting artificial intelligence and sending it far away. It all made sense.

Gilles and the RCMP had identified the way the boards were coming into the province—with Sparky's refurbs—but couldn't figure out how they were being shipped out. I was sure I could, and that I had. Those fishing boats Terry moored off orphan land were there to take the boards out to sea, and the larger ships that would carry them east.

But what was Murray's role?

I stopped walking to think.

The two men had known each other. It had been Murray who had told Terry how to evade tariffs by importing fabric and sewing here. That's who Murray was, what he did. An import-export trendspotter and enabler. And who better than an export entrepreneur to detect a smuggling operation? To want to get in on it? And who else but a genealogist with "I make sure" as an ancestral motto would be more likely to kill so that wouldn't happen?

Toby pulled on the leash. I started to move. I'd gotten it wrong about Louise. I couldn't do that again. I needed solid evidence to show that Murray had known about Terry's smuggling operation. How was I going to get that?

I needed help. I needed inspiration.

I needed ice cream.

So, as soon as we got home, I fed Toby and then headed off to Drummond.

The Foodmart was crowded. Close to the long weekend, locals were filling up with food for family who would be back for the holiday. Carts were full with early strawberries for shortcake, casserole supplies for late arrivals, and ingredients for whatever dish had been praised last time anyone was home. I steered through the crowd and muscled the stiff wheels of the cart into the outer aisle and the freezer compartment.

I was there, door open, cooling the aisle, trying to decide between chocolate and Moon Mist, a combination of banana, grape, and bubble gum, popular among those younger than the age of ten and the truly desperate, when I felt a jab between my shoulder blades.

"Valerie, my girl. Haven't seen you since the craft show. Hear you're up to something."

I turned around slowly, chocolate in one hand, Moon Mist in the other, and faced him.

"Up to something, Terry? I have no idea what you mean."

The tartan seller, historian, smuggler, and possible murderer smiled at me, his face sunburned by what must have been last week's twenty minutes of full sun. The tam on his head I knew, having done my research, was the Kirkpatrick tartan.

"The sewing," Terry said. "When I get up and running, Sheila Mackenzie was telling me, you or some of your Crafter's Co-op girls might be interested."

My hands were cold. I put both cartons in the cart and looked around for help in case I needed it. At the end of the aisle, a two-year-old was sliding out from between his mother's arms onto the tiled floor in a campaign for grape popsicles. The mother looked up and caught my eye. Neither one of us was having a reasonable day.

"Not at the moment, thanks. Maybe some other time," I said. *Like maybe after you are released at the end of 30 years in jail*, I thought. "But it's an interesting idea. Sheila says you're bringing in wool fabric to avoid the tariffs. Smart," I added, remembering my mother's advice that there were more bees to be gotten with honey than with vinegar.

"Hmm." Terry seemed annoyed. "You heard about that? Sheila's a talker, always was. I bring in as much as I can from my trips. The real stuff."

"Must keep you busy." I searched for something else to say. "But the tartans are not your only business, are they?" There it was. Right from my mind to my mouth. Unedited, as usual. Closer, the toddler had been gathered from his puddle on the floor and draped into the seat of his mother's shopping cart. His small legs were stiff, his face red. This was good. If the little boy went into temper-tantrum mode, the distraction would give me a chance to escape.

"You're right," Terry sighed, rocking his cart full of meat, potatoes, and canned soup as if it were a baby carriage. "Just doing what I have to do so I can pay the bills."

Wow. He was admitting it.

Louise had been a warm-up. This was, as Terry said himself, the real thing.

"Murray knew everything you had going on. Didn't he?" I asked. I was well beyond the point of no return. I looked down. Even the cartons of ice cream were sweating.

"You mean my genealogy?" Terry asked. "Not likely. He was interested in putting family crests on keychains, that's about it. No, I'm talking about deep research, family trees."

The toddler and mother were on their way to the cash register, negotiating for something. Most likely peace.

"Like you did for Moira, on the Frasers?" I stalled, hoping that the big workman in front of the butter display was heading in my direction. "I understand that what you found out helped her get an inheritance allowing her to start her restaurant." I would keep Terry talking until the man down the aisle was near, and then I would run out and call the RCMP.

"Say again?" Terry asked, astonished. "That's a stretch. I found some records in the National Records of Scotland and passed them on to her. She claims she followed them up and found some estate, but I wasn't involved in that. At least I got a plane ticket overseas out of the deal. I think she thought she was hiring an amateur. Someone who would bring back Fraser knickknacks for her decor. She should have known she was dealing with a trained archivist. But I found more than she bargained for."

This was not the direction I had thought this conversation was going to take. But it was also exactly where I had made a mistake with Louise. I hadn't listened. "What do you mean?"

"I looked at the original passenger manifest for the ship the *Hector*, as you would," he said. "And the man she said was her ancestor came with his wife but died a year later. There were no children. Whatever Moira's family tree is, that's not her branch."

The man from dairy saw me looking at him, and he winked. I turned back to Terry for one last try.

"Saltire Investments," I threw out. "It's you, isn't it?"

Terry stepped back. "Course not," he said. "Why would you think that? But I recognize the company."

A wife joined the man. She put his butter back in the case.

"You do?"

"Sure, I'm not going to forget a name like that, am I? It was at the bottom of the check. I cashed it fast, I can tell you."

"Hang on. What check?"

"Didn't I say?" Terry asked. "For the plane ticket to Edinburgh. That was the name printed on it. The one she gave me."

"Who are you talking about?"

"Moira Fraser. She's Saltire Investments."

CHAPTER TWENTY-TWO

A store employee reached past me and closed the door to the ice cream compartment. I had left it open, and frosty air drifted out into the aisle.

"Don't mind me," he said apologetically. "Got to think of the environment. Energy, things like that."

"Future generations," Terry agreed, assessing the man now positioned between us and the glass door. He moved his cart in closer, narrowing the channel for a conversational exit. "The legacy we leave," he began, preparing himself for a discussion of the millennium with the grocery clerk. "Generation after generation ... "

I interrupted.

"Terry. It was an open freezer. It's closed." I read the name tag on the pocket of the clerk's white shirt, next to his bright green clip-on bow tie. "Norm. We appreciate your help." I backed up my load of ice cream to open an escape for him. "But don't let us keep you."

I let Norm scurry off and then turned Terry.

"That's Moira's company? Are you sure?"

Terry seemed mystified by my interest. "Sure, I'm sure. I mean, anyone could have figured it out. Play on words. Salt. Salt Box. Saltire. She's got her theme. Kind of obvious." He glanced over at the checkout aisles. He spotted one of his regular customers with no one to talk to, waiting in the line with a basket of strawberries. "Nice seeing you, Val, but think I'll get a move on here. You good?"

I wasn't, but the reason why was more than I could explain to a meat-and-potatoes-eating tartan seller in the Foodmart.

"I'm great," I said, looking down at the softening cartons in my cart. "Time for me to go too. I have to get this home."

Terry nodded and hurried away to his next audience.

After he left, I realized I was now near the end of my search for information. I knew who was buying the orphan land; however, I still didn't know why. And my sense was that this part was the one that mattered. It might even explain why Murray had been killed. I doubted anyone else would recognize the connection between the two situations or be as familiar as I was with the people involved. That put me in the middle of this mess. Like it or not, I felt like a human point of intersection for many of the hidden stories active in the community. That gave me a responsibility to follow this through.

But how would I do that?

I had an idea. The best, and safest, place to check up on a restauranteur would be at her restaurant. In public, and not by myself. I needed someone to go with me. The last time I was at the Salt Box, it was with Stuart. I hadn't heard from him for a few days, which was unlike him, and unlike me.

I turned around and put the ice cream back into the freezer. I wouldn't need it now. I had a dinner date to set up.

I parked close to the Chinese restaurant. Above it were the offices of a dentist, a real-estate agent, a bookkeeper, and Stuart Campbell, Consulting Engineer. It was a beautiful early evening, the leaves on the trees covering the harsh bare branches of the winter months as if that season had never existed. The birds that had flown thousands of miles away in the fall had returned. Nature knew that everything worked out, and it believed in second chances. As I climbed the stairs to the second floor, I hoped Stuart would feel the same way.

The office at the end of the hall was quiet. The reception room, with its nautical maps on the walls, uncomfortable chairs, and coffee table covered in a fan of old sailing magazines, was empty. I walked through it and rapped on the frosted glass to an inner office.

"It's me," I said to the glass. "Do you have a minute?" I leaned closer to hear any voices, the sounds of a client or a meeting inside the room.

Suddenly, the door gave way, and I stumbled across the threshold.

"Valerie," Stuart sighed. "I was going to call you. We need to talk."

I straightened myself up, smoothed out my dress, then my hair, then my composure. "Same. That's why I'm here." I looked across at the papers, drawings, and volumes of building codes on Stuart's desk, and then to the maple mantlepiece clock on a shelf. "I haven't eaten. Do you have time to go out?"

Stuart smiled a smile that made me almost forget there was anything wrong between us. He reached for a Harris Tweed sports jacket hung on the back of the door. "For you, yes. Where do you want to go? Downstairs?"

He put his jacket on over his button-down shirt, one side of the collar over the lapel, one under. I reached over and straightened it out, like I always did.

"The Peking? No. I've been thinking of the salmon and potato cakes they serve at the Salt Box." I had remembered the note pinned on the menu the last time we were there. "It's Tuesday. The dinner special."

"Potato cakes? Done deal." Stuart motioned me through his just-for-show reception area, down the stairs, and out onto the street. "Let's walk," he said. "I hope this weather holds for the Sail By."

"About that," I ventured, aware I had to work into this and not let Stuart know how deep I was into solo investigations. "I found out who is behind Saltire Investments."

Stuart paused on the pavement. "What? You did? How did you manage that? Who are they?"

"It started out sewing-related," I said, implying the information had hunted me down on its own. "Fabric, quilted, recycled, and imported. And clan tartans. That was a big part of it." I searched the strip of grass between the sidewalk and the curb for inspiration. Yellow dandelions persistently occupied the space. I didn't consider any plant that cheerful a weed. "Do you have any idea how much wool it takes to make a kilt? A traditional one? Eight yards. That's a lot of pleating."

"You're stalling, Valerie." Stuart had an I-know-you look on his face that he had earned. "Where is this going? Who did you talk to?"

"Terry the Tartan," I said. "Terry Kirkpatrick. The careful, double-checking genealogist. The kind who would think to check the manifest of The *Hector.* And find out that there was no Fraser ancestor behind this restaurant." We had arrived. "The Salt Box."

Stuart looked at the arc of the sign painted in Celtic-style script on the window. "The Salt Box? Saltire? That's the connection?" I couldn't decide if Stuart was tired or resigned. "Not a lot to go on, Valerie."

"Please," I said. "I am only telling you what Terry told me. Moira in there"—I pointed into the dim restaurant—"bought Terry a plane ticket to go to Scotland and to research the Frasers who came to Nova Scotia. Mind you, all he found out was that she is an ordinary Fraser, not a founding-family one, but the ticket was paid for by Saltire Investments. The same outfit that's been buying up that random land."

Stuart was silent, but I could see the activity behind his eyes. He was making computations, ordering columns, pulling together facts in the spreadsheet of his mind. "The chart. Inside," he said. "I want to go back there and get another look at it." He reached out and took my arm. "Let's go."

When Moira saw us enter, she stopped chatting with two bright-eyed tourists seated at a front table and grabbed menus from a server's hand.

"I got this," she said to a young woman dressed in black pants, a white shirt, and a sash of Fraser tartan. "Val, Stuart, in for dinner? Let me seat you." She moved to a table near the window, but Stuart shook his head.

"I think we'd be happier down back," he said, motioning to a small table near the exit to the washrooms.

"I have lots of better tables," Moira protested.

"Down there's fine," he said, looking at me for help.

"We have to talk," I explained.

Moira looked at Stuart, and then at me, and then at Stuart again. A break-up meal, she seemed to decide. Close to the back door for a before-dessert getaway.

As we walked to the back of the room, we passed office parties of six or eight professionals with documents on the table, ready to sign before the Riesling wore off, and a few couples. These seemed evenly divided between older pairs focused on their plates and not each other and those at the courting stage, so busy presenting the best versions of themselves that they were unaware of what they ate.

Stuart and I were in a category of our own.

"What's going on?" I asked Stuart after Moira had seated us and we'd waived away the menus. Stuart faced the restaurant, back against the rear wall. "Why are we down here?"

Stuart leaned forward and held my hand. "Don't be obvious, but look what's on the wall behind me."

It was dim, but I could see a nautical chart, like many hung all around the restaurant. This one was yellowed, frayed around the edges, worn with crease marks made from many foldings. The ink itself was faded, but the outlines were still clear.

"It's old, but it looks to me like a drawing of the coast of the island," I reported. I could make out the lines of tiny waves and, on the land, the sketches of a few trees. It reminded me of the documents on Stuart's office walls, his antique engineering specifications, patents, and charts of the ocean. The older and the more detailed drawings were, the more likely he was to display them.

"Exactly," Stuart said. "I passed it last time we were here. There was something about that map that bothered me, something familiar. It's obviously a drawing of the area, but with marks made at specific little coves on the North Shore. I had a feeling that I knew what that meant, but I couldn't remember. Does that sound crazy?"

"I know feelings like that. Go on."

"Right. I woke up thinking again about it last night. I couldn't get back to sleep, so I went into my study. On the desk there was the drawing I did last time you and I were here. All the properties along the coast that had been bought up since the last Sail By. Do you remember it?"

"Of course I do." I looked at the map on the wall. "Do those marks on the map match the locations of the Saltire properties?" I asked. No wonder we were sitting back here.

"I think so," said Stuart. "This is important. From what you tell me, Moira has gone to a lot of trouble to hide her identity behind Saltire, and yet she has this map, drawn at least a hundred years ago, that I believe she's used to identify properties to buy, hung right here in her restaurant. But I can't say anything without confirmation, evidence."

I knew this was where I came in. "What do you want me to do?"

"Take a selfie, or whatever you call it, of our dinner when it arrives. The one thing Moira won't question is anyone photographing her food. When our dinner comes, I'd like you to stand up, take a picture of me and the plate, and then sneak in a shot of the map in the background. Do you think you can do that?"

"Of course I can do that," I said, holding up my phone in the iridescent-pink case Darlene had given me. "Who are you talking to? I live for intrigue, moments like this."

Stuart groaned. "Don't I know it." He squeezed my hand. "However, I've decided to just go along with it. Accept that's who you are."

"Might as well," I said. "That's what I've had to do."

The server arrived. I leaned back while she made room for our meal. Watercress and tiny heirloom tomatoes made a wreath around the rims of the plates, framing three sizable potato cakes flecked with chives next to a slab of pink salmon. Stuart examined the food as if it were a prop, which in this case it was, and then looked up at the server.

"Wine, maybe?" he asked. "Benjamin Bridge? Nova 7?"

He looked at me. "Two glasses?"

I nodded. The server wrote down this addition to our order and walked away.

"Nova 7?" I asked. "Not house white?"

"Photo op," Stuart said. He was warming to the adventure. I knew the sensation. "If I raise a glass, you can get a better shot of the full wall."

"Clever," I said. The server was back with two glasses. I took a sip, and we waited until she had retreated to the front of the restaurant. "Where's Moira?" I asked.

"At the cash register," Stuart said, sneaking a look. He pushed away from the table and hoisted his glass with a stiff smile. "Go. Now."

I realized how much I was enjoying this. In the few years we had known each other, this was the first time Stuart and I had been coconspirators. It felt like dancing, but with potato cakes and next to the women's washroom. In sync, operating together.

I took a lot of pictures. There were advantages to being an older woman. I made a show of struggling with the camera, stabbing it with an index finger, pretending I had messed up the shot and had to try again.

When I was done. I took a swig of my wine, sliced into my food, and handed Stuart my phone. He dropped his napkin into his lap and scrolled through.

"Good work, my love," he said absently. He usually called me Valerie, or Val. We had crossed some intimacy line. Being sneaky together does that to a couple. He swiped through the phone and then handed it back. He didn't resume eating but leaned back and looked at me silently.

"Well?" I said. Stuart was good at suspense. I had not known that about him.

"We've got it. Every mark on that map corresponds to each of those rocky little inlets, all five of them. All that Saltire Investments, and that would be Moira, owns."

"You're kidding. But what's going on?" I dropped my fork onto my plate. "Treasure. That's got to be it." I looked again at the chart on the wall behind Stuart's head. "It's a treasure map. Moira has this map. Maybe it was in her family, who knows with that one, and figured it out. She got this land because she can moor unregistered boats there and take the treasure away." I stopped. "But why would she go to so much trouble? I mean, to do it by boat?"

Stuart waited until a patron had entered and exited the washroom and passed our table before he answered me.

"Simple. Special Places Protection Act. By law, treasure hunters need a license, and any artifacts found are property of the province. That's got to be it," Stuart said. "She's found something and is sneaking it out on boats from unregistered moorings that no one can question because they are opposite her private land."

I'd finished my dinner.

"Who would have thought?" I asked. "I mean, the food's good here, which is something, when you consider cooking is her sideline."

"Probably hires local chefs," Stuart said. "But here's one thing I don't get. Why would anyone hang such a valuable document in the back of a busy restaurant?"

"Best place for it," I said. "Look at the walls, covered with old stuff. She turned it into decor. Best way to hide anything is to mix it in with the same." I had to admit it, Moira knew what she was doing. "Like Gilles in jail," I said to myself.

But not to myself.

"Excuse me. What did you say?" Stuart didn't need to ask, but he wanted me to repeat what I had just said. "Gilles? As in Gilles DeWolf? Have you heard from him?"

I was a good improviser, but a very poor liar. I knew that about myself. Just like I knew I had a voice that carried. I lowered it now.

"Yes. Not for long. Just the once. But I can't talk about it. I can't. It doesn't matter. It has nothing to do with you." The atmosphere in the room changed, like some sort of drain had opened in the floor and everything good about this day was spinning around and washing away.

Stuart wasn't looking at me anymore. Instead, he took his time arranging his cutlery in the center of his plate, as if he were performing surgery.

"Are you sure?" he said to his dinnerware. "I need you to be honest with me. What's going on with this guy?"

"Nothing. At least, nothing that affects you. Forget I said anything, it doesn't matter," I said. "It's not about you." I repeated.

Stuart threw his napkin onto his plate. "Not about me? Pay no attention that there's another man on the scene and you won't tell me anything about him? Me, the person with the first decent relationship he's had since his ex-wife left him with a toddler to go practice tax-haven law with her partner in Bermuda? Me, the guy who thought maybe this, with you, was it?" Stuart raised his face to me, and it was not angry as I expected, only hurt. "You can't talk about Gilles DeWolf, a criminal, who's back and you're meeting up with him? Even though he's, what did you say? In jail? What's going on?" He pointed to my phone with the picture of the chart still on it. "Are you part of this? Did you know this already? And what am I? Good old out-of-it Stuart? Again?" He pushed himself away from the table and got up.

"Don't go," I said. "I knew nothing about Moira or the map. Not anything more than you did until today." I wanted to tell Stuart everything but couldn't, not yet. "This isn't about us. But I promised, for someone's safety, not to talk about it. Not yet." Stuart started to walk away from the table. I reached out and put a hand on his arm. "I need you to trust me. Please. Can you do that?"

Stuart stood still and looked at my hand until it dropped away.

"I'll pay the bill," he said. "On the way out. You don't owe me anything."

CHAPTER TWENTY-THREE

A diner walked by me to the washroom. Moira was right about one thing: This wasn't a good table. The woman passed Stuart on his way out. She looked at me with a question on her face. *The break-up table, I know,* I wanted to say to her. I reached over for what was left in Stuart's wineglass and drained it.

"There's lots of fish in the sea," the woman said, sympathetic and, this being Nova Scotia, unable to mind her own business.

I nodded, because it was better than trying to explain or crying.

I had to get out of there.

Out on the sidewalk, I saw I wasn't the only one making a getaway. Halfway back to my car, a gray van with "The Salt Box" on its side drove past me. Moira was leaving her restaurant. During the dinner rush. Not long after I had taken photos of that map and Stuart had left.

Moira was taking care of business. Nothing, I was sure, that had anything to do with nouvelle Scottish cuisine.

She would not get away with it. I'd had enough of waiting. I needed this to be done. Only then could I tell Stuart everything. Only then would he understand.

This was my chance to bring this nightmare to an end.

I got into my car, snapped on my seatbelt, and used the system Stuart had set up for me to talk on the phone while I drove.

It rang a few times before he picked up.

"Jeff? It's Valerie Rankin again. Can we talk?"

"Absolutely. What can I do for you?"

"Remember, you were going to check that film you took of the Salt Box booth at the show?"

"Ah, right. Yes, sorry. I'm on another job at the plastics business in the old fish plant. I have it out in the truck."

"Okay, great. You're at work. I'll let you go. But would you mind swinging by, say, tomorrow at the store—you know, Rankin's General—and let me have a look?" I wanted to talk to Jeff and thought he might be more comfortable meeting me at a business.

I could almost hear Jeff's unspoken thoughts about a middle-aged busybody interrupting real work on a real day.

"I don't see why you would want to see it," he said, slowly. "You asked me something about a heater ... I'm not sure it's even in the shots. Condiments maybe, Miss Fraser smiling. A few of the other booths. Mostly pretty dull stuff."

"I can imagine, but as a favor, can I look at the video myself? I'd appreciate it," I said. "I want to be sure of something." I didn't know what I was looking for, but I was sure I would know it if I saw it.

Jeff gave up. He had things to do. "Alright then. Later," he said. "At the store."

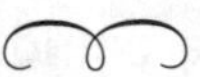

I knew from the direction Moira's van was headed where she was going.

The causeway. I headed there myself now, taking a shortcut long-time locals would know, but someone who had come here from away might not. I turned down a backstreet; past an intersection known as the Willow Tree, even though that tree had been cut down a generation ago; and onto a one-way street that became a two-way exactly when I needed it. I made it to the outside lane onto the causeway only a few car lengths across from oblivious Moira in her van. I ducked behind an eighteen-wheeler and hoped she hadn't seen me.

The lights changed. The truck ahead snorted to a stop. It was a big one, the refrigerated kind, full of seafood, with "From Down East to the Far East" painted across the back doors. I knew the lights ahead had changed when all the brakes required for eighteen wheels were released.

I stayed behind the truck, but on the twists and turns up the side of Gasper's Island, I kept Moira in view.

She was going exactly where I had expected she'd go, no doubt to check on the five properties marked on her treasure-trove chart. If I was very lucky, I would see which one she went to, and then I'd call in the RCMP. The scale of this operation, and its personal cost, was too much for me. I needed to turn the whole thing over to Wade, Nolan, and even Gilles, and then I could back out.

Even still, I didn't want to get too close to Moira. After all, she must have killed Murray, the interfering entrepreneur, at a busy craft show with hundreds of possible witnesses.

That took nerve. If Moira could do that, I didn't like my chances alone with her on a deserted coastline.

At the top of the hill, the eighteen-wheeler between her van and my car turned onto a side road. I pulled back, hoping Moira didn't see me as she barreled ahead. Right past each of the properties that she had purchased.

I wasn't expecting this. I was so sure Moira had left to check on her treasure sites.

So, where was she going now? Was she meeting someone?

Confused, I sped up and took the next bend. I was just in time to see Moira's van take a hard left turn I knew well.

Her destination was the Gasper's Cove Yacht Club.

It was a private club, but a public lot. I'd be safe there. I parked as far away from Moira's van as I could. I was too late to see in which direction she had gone. I'd start at the most official building, the clubhouse and bar.

The dining room, a dozen tables surrounded by more captain's chairs than could fit comfortably around them, was empty. Unlike Moira's restaurant in town, the yacht club only opened for dinner, mostly of the deep-fried kind, on weeknights. I knocked on the manager's door, and no one answered. Then, I heard sounds in the kitchen.

Moira was alone at the long counter, her back to me, a brown-paper envelope on the wooden cutting board in front of her, as she unpacked a cloth shopping bag full of jars.

When she heard me come into the room through the swinging doors, Moira turned around to face me.

"Valerie? What are you doing here? Weren't you just having dinner at my restaurant?"

"I was. But I left. Like you did."

Suspicion crossed Moira's face. "Are you saying you followed me?"

There seemed to be no point in denying it.

"Think I did."

"Why? I'm dropping off a catering proposal for a function and some condiments." She gestured to the brown envelope on the cutting board and the jars. "How is that any of your business?"

The first reason that came to mind was the truth.

"I wanted to see if you were checking on your treasure-exporting operation."

"What? And what were you going to do with that information?"

I couldn't believe it. The woman hadn't even tried to deny it. How was I going to get the RCMP here so she could say the same thing to them?

"I was going to blow the whistle," I said, aware that when I tried to talk like someone else, even when it seemed appropriate, I embarrassed myself.

"Who sent you?"

I noticed she thought I couldn't do any of this myself.

"Who do you think?" I asked. "You tell me." I thought this tactic was very clever, but then again, I had to buy time. Murray obviously hadn't been careful, and look what had happened to him.

"It's the French, isn't it?" Moira snarled.

I stepped back. This situation was moving faster than I had expected. It also looked like DeWolf's arrival in town was not the secret he and the RCMP thought it was.

"I'll never tell them where," she said. "Never."

"You don't have to," I said. "Not when you have it posted on the wall of your restaurant. Anyone who has to use the bathroom can see it."

I had Moira there.

She, however, had her hand on the carving knife next to her envelope on the wooden block. This was a good time to distract her.

"Saltire is you," I said. "The name gave it away."

"You mean the seasoning? You could taste it?"

I wondered if Moira was losing her mind. That would explain a lot. Like murder.

"It's not going to work to try to change the subject," I said. "The land. You bought useless property from the municipality because the mayor's desperate for money. You knew that was where the treasure was hidden. You wanted mooring so boats could come in and carry it out. Just like the rumrunners, wasn't it? You'll move out anything for money. Artifacts that belong to the province." I paused, a new and brilliant idea lighting up my mind. "And circuit boards for AI that aren't supposed to leave the continent. You're just a young, modern, nouvelle-cuisine version of Al Capone."

There. I'd said it.

Moira put the knife down, but then she picked up a cleaver. This was not an improvement.

"What are you talking about?" she asked. "I'm not smuggling. I'm running a perfectly legitimate business. I just don't want anyone to know where I got it."

"What do you mean?"

"Salt," Moira said. "Salt Box? Saltire?" She studied my face as if looking for some click of understanding on my face. When she didn't see that, she continued. "You know nothing about the competitive world of fine cuisine, do you? Fine evaporated salt?"

I was offended. I was moving on from tuna casseroles. Among Gasper's Cove housekeepers, I was not the worst cook.

"Maybe not. But what does that have to do with anything?" I asked.

"Everything," Moira said. "Maybe the heritage detail in my brand isn't entirely accurate, but that chart is. When my family came to the area, they did what everyone else did. They preserved their food, fish, in salt, a practice that required large quantities of it. It was like gold to them, more precious than any treasure. And it happens that the Gasper's Cove coastline has places with small pools in the granite that are naturally ideal locations for collecting high-density, high-saline, seawater. The kind that produces a world-class, distinctive sea salt when evaporated. Too precious for preserving, but just as valuable, if not more so, as a finishing salt. When I understood that the old chart marked these pools, naturally I wanted to buy the land next to them."

"To evaporate salt? But why the boats? You don't need them for evaporation."

"No, you don't, but you need them for secrecy. You have no idea how cutthroat the food world is right now. I decided the safest, most undetectable, way to produce my salt was on location. We do it all on board. We run plastic pipes from the pools and, using the bilge pumps, bring it to tanks with the technology to expedite the evaporation process. When the salt's ready, we pack it and ship it out—through customs, by the way, perfectly legitimate." Moira put down her cleaver. I could see then that like I was with a pair of fabric shears, she thought better with her tools in her hand.

I pulled a kitchen chair toward me and sat down.

"You're not a smuggler?" I asked. One last time, to make sure. "And you didn't murder Murray?"

"No, I am not a gangster, and I didn't kill anyone," she said. "I'm just a girl with a very good family history who likes to cook."

CHAPTER TWENTY-FOUR

This time, I didn't follow Moira's van when she left the yacht club.

She'd explained more than any sewing teacher needed to know about artisan salt there in the kitchen, and after that, I had apologized. Once I had adjusted to the idea that salt was a serious business, her explanation made sense. I'd seen Himalayan sea salt down at the Foodmart. If anyone would climb those mountains to extract and export that, the idea of accessing salt pools in Nova Scotia didn't seem so far-fetched. Small fishing boats were perfect for the job too. They could get close to shore, had flat spaces in the hull for evaporation equipment, and could travel down the coast and be unloaded without attracting attention. Moira's salt-harvesting operation was simple, smart, and apparently very lucrative. The inheritance that had launched the restaurant had come not from any estate in Scotland but from the information recorded in an old document here at home.

But losing Moira as a suspect was disappointing. I admitted to myself that I had no idea what to do next. I had been given too many secrets to hold and no one to share them with. I needed Stuart, but I had hurt him. I didn't mean to, but I had. My cousin Darlene, my aunt Colleen, and Duck couldn't be told what I had to say. Jimmy had his own troubles, and I was only getting to know him. I had nothing for Nolan or Wade. And the sad truth was that the only person I could talk to about any of this, Gilles DeWolf, was both in jail and not to be trusted.

I was out of options, support, and ideas. The only choice I had was to drive away from the yacht club, open the car window, and release my worries to the breeze and the ocean.

I did that, and a whisper in the wind, an answer, came back to me.

I remembered.

The video.

Jeff's video. He had said he would bring it by the store tomorrow.

But why wait another day? He was at a job, at the old fish plant.

I was almost there. I thought I saw a light in the dark. It was late, but maybe ...

How could it hurt?

I was in the neighborhood. I thought I'd drop by, ask to see the video, save him some trouble.

The building was around the next corner.

I flipped on my indicator and made the turn.

The only vehicle parked in front of the converted fish plant was Jeff's truck. I parked and walked up to the building's front door. I considered knocking, but this wasn't a house, so I walked in.

I'd been inside before, as a teenager. One summer during university, I had been one of the crew who stood there in stained white coats, rubber boots, and hairnets, grabbing and packing the cod, haddock, halibut, mackerel, crab, and lobster as it moved past us on the wet conveyor belts.

But that was a long time ago. Those fish-plant workers were gone, made redundant by onboard processing, replaced by machines, eliminated by packaging. The crates and boxes used to ship live seafood were the work of this building now.

The open area was bright, illuminated by hanging lights dropped down from the flat ceiling. At one end of the building were the factory's ingredients, plastic boards filed on their sides like cookie sheets and open vats of pellets ready to be fed into the enormous ice-cube tray molds beneath the huge presses. Far at the back were the finished containers themselves, stacked on pallets near the loading deck, like rows and rows of giant lunch boxes.

And next to these was the only other human in the room, Jeff the videographer.

I couldn't see his camera or his gear. I looked along the walls. There, I saw mousetraps. I could smell mothballs, scattered to keep rodents away.

Ahead of me, near the loading dock, a clipboard in his hand, Jeff was counting boxes.

I walked down toward him.

"Jeff!" I called out.

He spun around. "Valerie? How did you get in here?"

"The door was open." We were in a room full of plastic boxes. What did it matter? "I was passing by, and I thought maybe you could show me the video, if you have a moment."

"Video?" Jeff slid his clipboard between two stacked rows of containers, out of sight. "What video?"

How could he have forgotten? I stopped beside a long table. On it were what looked to be the insides of a cooler, next to a tile-size board covered in aluminum mesh. I picked it up. It felt light. "What's this? Looks like the filter to the exhaust fan over my stove."

Jeff moved closer to me. Aggression rippled toward me, catching me off guard.

"Give that to me." Jeff held out his hand. "You have no idea what that is."

He was wrong.

I was a person who talked. Listened. Remembered. Who had been in this fish plant when that's what it was.

"There are plenty of fish in the sea." The woman at the restaurant had said it in passing, and she was right. But these days, many were processed on the big trawlers. Packed on board and sent on for exporting.

I stood there and was aware of Jeff watching me. As if he could see the fragments of many conversations flying across the inside of that big empty building to me, all fitting together, like pattern pieces for a dress. Making sense, finally, of what had happened and what now could happen to me. I said out loud what we both knew.

"This isn't an exhaust-fan filter, is it? It's a Gideon board." Jeff's eyes flicked. It was as good as a nod. "I've heard they are used in producing artificial intelligence. Someone told me that these boards"—I held it up—"are like gold, but the factories offshore can't get them." I pointed to the boxes stacked by the back door. "You're hiding them in the walls of these seafood boxes, aren't you?" Like the words on the truck, From Down East to the Far East. A good seamstress notices details. "Seafood packaged here, moved to Halifax airport, and sent to Asia."

Jeff was still, like a cat. One gathered into himself, ready to jump.

"Very smart." I kept talking. "Tricky. Got to give you that."

Vanity flickered across Jeff's face. I saw his weakness and used it, trying to buy myself time.

"Did Murray set this up, and you took over? You figured you could do a better job?"

"Excuse me?" Jeff took a step forward. I tried to visualize the route to the door behind me. If I made a run for it, would I make it? "This was *my* operation," he said. "Murray got around. He was in and out of many businesses in the area. I needed a front for the export side of my operation. I used Murray. These promos I filmed for him gave me a reason to walk through the doors he opened, to see if any of them had what I needed."

"Why here?"

Jeff couldn't resist the chance to explain how clever he was, or maybe he'd decided that I would never make it out to tell anyone.

"The location is perfect," Jeff said. "When Murray told me about an island called 'Last Gasp,' with lobster, I knew I had a winner. This is the last place anyone would expect to find a first-class operation."

That's what you think, I thought. I know one ex-Mountie, currently wearing a set of orange scrubs and eating food below his standards, who knew that this was *exactly* where to look. Gilles knew better than to underestimate us; Jeff didn't.

The loading-dock door behind Jeff was slightly open. Briefly, through it, I saw a flicker of headlights, on and then off, as if someone had pulled in and parked. The RCMP? How did they know to come here? I didn't care.

"Import and export," I said like a rhyme, stalling. "It seems everyone's talking about that these days. I understand how you used these containers to ship the boards out. But how did you get the Gideons here in the first place? High-tech electronics are the one thing we don't make here in Gasper's Cove."

Jeff laughed. "Getting the boards in was easy. Cheap electronics with 'refurbished' parts." He made air quotes around the words. That move usually annoyed me, but I let it pass. "There's a Sparky in every community, a small-time contractor cutting corners. The units came in, and he snapped out the Gideons and sent them to a Nova Scotia address. He was told he was forwarding the returns. Then, he had one of his boys put cheap boards in the units we brought in from the US."

"Creative," I said. Most of the time, I admired nothing more. This time, I wasn't so sure.

"Thank you." Jeff took the compliment. "This plastics outfit was ready to sell, and Murray set it up, not knowing I was the buyer. I had the specs for the containers made up by some people I know."

There was nothing more to say.

Jeff's hand went into his pocket, and he pulled out a Taser. Both Nolan and Wade carried them. I knew what they were and what they could do.

"Shocks are your thing, aren't they?" I asked. My filter was long gone. "Murray's pacemaker didn't go off because of any old heater, or anything Jimmy did. It was you, wasn't it? With that?"

Jeff didn't answer my questions. He didn't have to. His smile did. The Taser raised in his hand, Jeff took one step toward me. I knew what would happen next. I'd be out cold in the old fish plant while the second criminal mastermind I'd known, and not the one who was charming, or French, made his escape.

I braced myself and closed my eyes. I felt trapped, like a patient in a dentist's chair, ready to be hurt.

And then, as I stood waiting to hear the click of a Taser in his hand, the metal door behind Jeff grated to the side, and the doorway was filled by a familiar silhouette.

I held my breath.

"Val," Nancy Mullins shouted. "I was on my way home from a bridal shower and saw you were ahead of me on the road. I followed you here. I was hoping you'd help me set up something between Heidi and Jimmy MacNeil. Thought I'd come in this way."

Jeff swiveled his head around while keeping me in his sights. "You? You're kidding." He lowered his arm with the Taser and held it tight against his body.

Nancy walked into the fish plant, now a plastics factory, as if this were the most normal place for her to be this late.

She considered Jeff, ignored his attitude, and regrouped. "A dance. Maybe you'd be interested too," she said to him nimbly. "There's a social in Drummond. This Saturday night. Live band, should be a good time." She paused, having done her selling, to close the deal. "No need to go alone. Come to think of it, I have the girl for you."

Stunned, I watched Nancy snap open a briefcase-size handbag, rifle through it, and pull out a photo. She held it up. I recognized the hairnet: Rosie from the Foodmart. "Nice face, good family," she said, then paused, as if digging for more of the supermarket cashier's other good qualities. "Light on her feet. Good dancer." With still no reaction from Jeff, she pulled out her best. "Makes a lovely ham and scalloped-potato casserole," Nancy added, with a wink.

For a moment, Jeff, the head of an international electronics-smuggling operation involving at least half the globe, and at least one murder I knew of, was at a loss for words.

I knew this was my chance.

CHAPTER TWENTY-FIVE

In that one moment, when Jeff was distracted by Nancy, I reached into my pocket and pulled out my own deadly weapon.

It was a new seam ripper; I went through a lot of them, and it was sharp. The Taser worried me. I had to deal with that. And this was a good seam ripper, of the old-school type, razor sharp, with a tiny red ball on the top of the hook, the rest of it capable of slicing through topstitching on jeans, rows of serged loops, or the veins on a wrist.

I lunged at Jeff, aiming for the hand with the weapon. The seam ripper connected. The Taser hit the floor. Dazed, Jeff grabbed his arm and spun around, gathering himself to take a run at me.

But then, Nancy stepped between us, and with the practiced agility of a woman who had fought her way through many estate sales, grabbed the Taser that had skidded to her feet, picked it up, and pointed it at Jeff. I was, at that moment, almost certain Nancy had no idea what a

Taser was, but I did know she could work a rural auction. She knew how to bluff.

"That's enough there, buddy boy," she said. "Me and my friend Val are going out that door. It looks like you haven't been behaving yourself." She paused and looked at Jeff; his arm was raised, held up with his good hand at the elbow. Blood streamed down his sleeve.

"You're going to need a tourniquet on that," she said matter-of-factly. She pulled a watercolor-print silk scarf free from her neck and waved it in front of the injured videographer and smuggler, as if taunting a cat. "If you don't try to stop us from leaving, you can have this."

"You wouldn't," Jeff said. I could see his assessment of us, two middle-aged women, and the calculations behind his eyes. I could also see that the blood from Jeff's wrist was flowing freely. He noticed that too.

"We would do it, and we are," Nancy said, backing away, armed with a Taser she didn't know how to use, beside me, with a silk scarf, worn, but of good quality, with a rolled hem, hand done.

Jeff took a step toward us but stopped. His face was pale. The blood on the concrete floor at his feet rolled toward a drain installed in the building's fish-plant days.

We kept walking toward the way I had come in, our eyes locked with those of a man who had caused so much trouble.

When we felt the door to the outside behind us, Nancy motioned to the door handle. I tied the scarf to it with a double knot. Jeff would need that scarf more than he would need to catch us.

That done, we crashed the door open and were through.

"Run," Nancy yelled at me. "My car, around the back, the Mustang. A widow gave me a good price, eight cylinders. Fast."

We ran past Jeff's truck. The window was down. Nancy reached inside, opened the door, and the interior light went on.

"What are you doing?" I shrieked.

"Keys." She held up a ring and handed them to me. "Let's get out of here."

The tires of the Mustang spun as Nancy took a fast turn out onto the main road. She drove like a race car driver, down the Shore Road and toward town. I tightened my seat belt and pulled out my phone. I was halfway through my message to the 911 operator when Nancy interrupted. "The paramedics," she said. "Say to send them too."

She was right.

I added that information and then hung up.

"What do we do now?" I asked. I wasn't sure exactly when this had happened, but Nancy was the lead in this operation. There was nothing ordinary about ordinary women, particularly not the one in the driver's seat beside me. The Taser was in the cupholder between us. I put Jeff's keys beside it. I started to talk, but Nancy lifted her fingers.

"Let me think," she said. "Okay. We go straight to the Mounties. They need to know what happened." She took her eyes off the road for a second to look at me. "Nice work with the seam ripper."

"It pays to get a good one," I said, as if I were talking to a sewing class. "The cheap ones aren't sharp enough." I realized how awful this sounded. "For stitches," I added, remembering the blood. The seam ripper was in my pocket. I didn't think I'd use it again. "I hope he'll be alright."

We rounded a hill. Two sets of headlights were already on their way over to the island from Drummond.

"Ah, he'll be fine," Nancy said. Two RCMP cruisers came off the causeway and rushed past us, sirens on. "Although, like a lot of tough guys, underneath, he isn't."

I couldn't believe what had just happened or what I had done. "It's amazing you showed up when you did," I said. "Heaven knows what Jeff would have done if I had been alone with him. Thank you."

"Don't mention it," Nancy said. "I was driving by and saw your car and his truck. I thought it wouldn't hurt to stop and have a word. It all turned out for the best. Except maybe for Rosie. She's a nice girl. But that guy is definitely not a good prospect."

CHAPTER TWENTY-SIX

When Nancy and I walked into the RCMP detachment in Drummond the next morning, Dawn Nolan came out to meet us.

"Boy, you guys were some fast last night," Nancy complimented the officer. "We passed the cruisers and an ambulance coming down the Shore Road. Lightning speed. I'd hardly hung up with 911."

"That's because we were already on our way out," Nolan said. "We knew all about Jeff before you called. That you'd attacked him was new, though. A seam ripper, I understand; he told the paramedics. That's got to be a first."

I reached into my pocket, pulled out my weapon, and handed it to Nolan. "You'll probably want this," I said. "Evidence?"

Nolan waved the seam ripper aside. "No need. The paramedics say he's going to be fine. And I have a feeling he's not going to press charges."

Nancy stepped in front of me, with a sideways glance at the junior officer at the desk. When she saw the solitaire on the young woman's finger, she shrugged and spoke to Nolan. "Self-defense. I was there. But I got to say, I would appreciate a little background on this situation. What's going on?"

Nolan sighed. She waved for us to follow her down the hall. "Come on. Given what you two ladies have been through, you deserve at least some kind of explanation." Nancy walked into the room first. Nolan stopped me to put a hand on my arm.

"Our mutual friend is the source of some of the information I'm about to share." She paused to make sure I understood that this was a reference to Gilles, and then she continued. "The one you never met."

"Got it," I said, pretending to zip my mouth and throw away the key. "Where is he now?"

"Somewhere else," Nolan said. I detected her relief. "You don't need to know where." She studied me. "He won't be back."

Dawn Nolan was glad Gilles was gone. But not half as much as I was. That man thought he understood me. But he had no idea. None at all.

It took us the best part of an hour to hear the parts of Jeff's story that Nolan could share. It might have taken less time if she had been explaining it to someone other than me and Nancy.

"Let me get this straight," I said, trying to interpret the more technical parts of Jeff's scheme. "It's possible to pack lobsters up at sea, seal them, and fly them right to Asia with no one checking on them?"

Nancy fielded this question herself. "Live lobster, remember that, Val. Those little things got to make it right across the world in one piece. Temperature-controlled boxes. Know all about it. One of my girls married a fellow on a boat."

Nolan looked confused.

"A matchmaking client," I explained.

"Right." Nolan backed her chair away from the table, just a bit. "Thirty-five to 45 degrees Fahrenheit, 2 to 7 Celsius, controlled by electronic sensors. The catch is packed at sea between gel packs in temperature-controlled containers. Foam-insulated walls. The old fish plant was being used to fabricate packaging with the illegal circuit boards sandwiched in the walls."

I could visualize it. "So, even if the containers were X-rayed by security at the airport, and anyone saw something electronic inside, they'd have no way of knowing it shouldn't be there for the temperature thing?"

"Correct," Nolan said.

"Airport?" Nancy asked. "Is that how they got them out?"

"Yes," Nolan said. "Believe it or not, there's a legitimate airline that flies out of Halifax airport, and that's all they do. Those lobsters have their own 747s. Boat, to plane, to Asia, sealed the whole way so there is no spoilage. They call it cold-chain logistics. The emphasis is on maintaining a consistent temperature in the containers, not on what they contain."

"'From Down East to the Far East,'" I said. "I saw the trucks. I can't believe it. Right in broad daylight, written on the side of an eighteen-wheeler. Who would have thought?"

"No kidding," Nancy said. "But Officer Nolan, where did you get all this information? Not from Jeff."

Nolan glanced at me quickly, then looked away. "We've been building up a background picture from many sources. But it was someone local who figured it all out. I can say it now—that Jimmy MacNeil is pretty sharp. Jimmy was curious and got a look at one of the so-called warranty boards. He took a picture."

I was finally catching on. "It was one of those Gideon-board things, am I right?" I asked. "But how would an electrician in Gasper's Cove, even a good one, know what one of those looked like?"

"Jimmy uploaded the picture for identification and showed it to Stuart," Nolan explained. "Apparently, it took a minute to get the answer with AI."

"AI? Do we know them?" Nancy asked me.

"It's not a person. AI. Artificial intelligence," I told her. Ironically, the same technology that had undone Gilles's art-forgery enterprise.

"Right. A pretend person. I get it," Nancy said. "But the lobster shipments. How did that get figured out? And how did you know it was Jeff?"

"Stuart made that connection," Nolan said. "He did some work on converting the fish plant for light manufacturing. Murray organized the contract. Stuart said he once asked Murray, why go to the trouble of manufacturing the shipping containers locally, when they were easy to buy anywhere? Jeff was there, and he stepped in and said, 'Quality.' Stuart remembered thinking this was strange, that the guy who was there to shoot film was acting like it was his own business."

"Because it was," I said. "But how did Stuart go from that to figuring out the rest of it?"

Nolan laughed. "You'll have to ask him. But I gather it was because of you."

"Me? How?"

"Something about the way you get when you think you're 'on the case.' His words, not mine. Murray's death rattled everyone, and Stuart was concerned you'd get yourself in trouble of some kind. He got it in his head that if he could get to the bottom of whatever was going on before you did, he could protect you."

"Protect Val?" Nancy laughed. "Someone should tell that boy this one can take care of herself. Never leaves home without her seam ripper."

I didn't say anything to that.

Because it was true.

CHAPTER TWENTY-SEVEN

Sewing class started late the next night. My students had so much to say, it was hard to settle them down.

I couldn't blame them.

"There's something you should know." Two expert quilters and half-hearted T-shirt makers, a mother and her daughter-in-law, pulled me aside to a corner of the classroom, away from the hanging steam iron. "Your classes have put us off garment sewing," the mother-in-law said.

"Yeah. Right off," her daughter-in-law said. "No offense."

"None taken," I responded, which was a lie. "Any reason?"

"It's not relaxing," the mother-in-law explained. "Quilting is sort of, what do you call it, meditative?"

"Zen," her daughter-in-law contributed. "Get in the zone. Stitch, press, stitch, repeat, and repeat. Once you've planned a quilt out, there's not a lot of pressure. We're thinking of getting our own booth for the fall show. Traditional bed quilts. What we know how to sew. Go into our own business, kind of."

"No more piecework?" I asked.

"None," the younger woman said. "But that lady from New York has her samples, at least. Paid us good, and that's it, we're done."

"Done like a dinner. But I feel bad for Terry," her mother-in-law admitted. "He was going to hire us next."

Nancy joined us. "I wouldn't worry too much," she smiled. "Haven't you heard? He and Sheila are going to work together. She'll sew, he'll sell. A widow and a widower." Nancy nudged Heidi next to her. "One thing can lead to another. Am I right? Just make yourself available."

Heidi's fair skin turned pink.

"Any chance you can knit?" Nancy asked casually. "There's a group, all men, who meet at the church ... "

Colleen stepped in. "Nancy, stop it. I am sure the girl's got enough going on at work."

This was my cue.

"That's right. The mayor was over to talk to us about an idea he and Darlene cooked up. Louise started it, something about a 'promotional hook' for the launch of a thing for the fall called the 'Fisherman's Aesgthetic.' When it's time, he's putting the town online. We're going to post pictures of us dressed the way we are, doing what we do. The Crafter's Co-op is going to be part of it, with an expanded online store. Gasper's Cove is going to be 'social proof' for the collection."

"Social proof?" the mother-in-law quilter asked. "What in the world is that?"

"Examples people can follow. Sort of the how-tos on being the real thing." Heidi pulled her phone from her back pocket and read the draft description on the municipality's new home page. "'A Coastal Community with a Laid-Back Vibe.'" She put her phone down. "Providing social proof means that every one of us is going to be an influencer. Authorities on how to be us. If you know who you are, you don't need to buy it, but not everyone is that lucky. Some of them do."

"That's right. No middlemen," I said, and then regretted it, hoping no one would think it a slur on poor Murray, who had not lived to see what would come next. "We're going global on our own," I added, picking up my scissors; it was time we got sewing. "And best of all, we don't have to leave here to do it."

When the last student left after class, I stayed in the classroom for the peacefulness of it. My favorite time in the store was at night. In the quiet, empty of customers and activity, the old building spoke to me. It shared with me the memory of trees in its timbers, of bending under ocean winds and time. It told me its stories, of generation after generation of one family, one island, one place. It closed around me like a hug, holding me safe like a mother, a grandmother, an ancestor. It shared with me the messages that they had sent forward into the future, comfort for any of us who one day might need it.

Like I did now, the Rankin who had tried to do things right but had gotten it wrong.

I shared the whole story with the old building. Of Jeff's arrest at the hospital. I told the listening walls about Murray and Louise, ambitious people without a clan behind them. I told them about Moira, who had inherited salt pools, and of Terry, who had inherited history. I shared the secret skill of Duck's fair-isle socks and explained about Jimmy, who had been so underestimated, mostly by himself.

The store was so quiet, listening, that I almost didn't hear the sound of the door to the back landing opening. The steady steps walking down the aisle, past Colleen's counter at the front, to stop at the open door of the classroom.

"I knew this would be where you were," he said. "We have to talk."

CHAPTER TWENTY-EIGHT

"What are you doing here?" He had startled me.

Stuart walked into the classroom. He checked to make sure the iron was unplugged and sat down. He answered my question with one of his own.

"Are you ever going to lock that back door when you're in here by yourself?" he asked.

"Maybe," I said, then stepped off the cliff, hoping it wasn't going to lead to a fall. "You wanted to talk?" I wanted to talk; I always did. But this time, I had no idea what I'd say, only a sense that whatever it was, it had to be the right thing.

"I did," Stuart said. "Nolan gave me some background, the part I didn't know. About how you and Jimmy were keeping your eyes open in the community while the RCMP worked on closing down this smuggling operation. I understand why neither of you could tell me about it. You had no choice. I thought you did, but you didn't. I'm sorry. I know I flew off the handle at you, but I wasn't thinking straight."

I moved over to the chair next to Stuart and put my arm around his shoulders. "It's okay. You had no way of knowing. Forget about it."

"Thanks," Stuart said, leaning into me. "But here's the thing. I was so wound up about you not trusting me enough to tell me about DeWolf, that I lost sight of the fact that you were the one who asked to be trusted, and I let you down."

"Let me down? You did not."

"I did. And you know why? I was jealous." Stuart studied the worn boards on the floor. "Who'd trust someone with a name like that with a woman they are in love with?"

This was a conversation I didn't want to rush. I liked the way it was going. "Gilles? You're kidding. That man is a walking, talking line. That one would lie about lying, and he probably did."

"You mean that?" Stuart asked. "No attraction on your side, none at all?"

"Look, Stuart. You know everything about me, and it's still all fine with you. You even know things about me I don't even know about myself. I can be myself with you. Let me tell you, if any human being can find that in another person, even once in their life, it's a miracle. You are my miracle."

"You mean that?"

I put my head on Stuart's shoulder. He smelled of soap and the onions he had chopped while making his daughter's dinner. He had the scent of the little dog he had walked along the ocean on him, and of the spring of last year, and the spring of the next. He was everything Gilles DeWolf could never understand, or be.

"Of course I mean that," I said. "There's nothing like a phony to make a woman appreciate the real thing."

What happened next, the day of the Gasper's Cove Yacht Club's annual Sail By, no one would ever believe. Not even if we told them, which we did not.

Not one of us. Not a woman, a man, a child, or a smart-enough-to-speak dog.

It was our secret.

And we kept it.

The conspiracy required no organization. The word had gone out through the usual broadcast channels, and that was enough. It was shared over early-morning coffee at the Agapi restaurant, muttered between the fishermen at the wharf, mentioned in passing in my sewing classes, phoned out by Nancy from her armchair headquarters at home, tucked into shopping bags and handed to local customers by my aunt Colleen at the front counter at our store. It was part of the quiet chat in the line at the Foodmart, tossed in between talk about the weather by dog walkers, passed ear to ear between parents waiting outside schoolyards, and slipped in between knitted stitches by the Men with Sticks.

We knew exactly what we needed to do.

No explanation was necessary. It was a deal sealed silently and by agreement. The location of the salt pools would remain Moira's family secret, as her ancestors had intended. We would protect it, for them, for her, for us, and for the nesting plovers.

In return, Moira opened viewing access to the islanders on her bits of precious property so they could watch the spring boats as they sailed by, as they had always done. And there she stood, among us, knowing continuity was community, as her forebearers had known. Sparky Bailey contributed fairy lights for the bushes, and those looked pretty from the boats.

I wasn't onshore myself.

My own view was of the water as it was parted by the bow of Stuart's sailboat, as it led the procession of anything in Gasper's Cove that could float, decorated with balloons, streamers, nautical flags, and yards and yards of tartan. Around the island we went, passing the crowds. I saw small groups on the shore. I thought I saw Jimmy with a girl who looked a little like Heidi, but I wasn't sure.

We had the dogs, Birdie and Toby, with us, wearing doggie life jackets. Together, they lifted their noses to the wind, to the salt, to detect the scent of real freedom the way only animals can.

And so, Stuart and I sailed, not by but back to where we had come from. It was the first time we had captained together.

But it would not be our last.

THE END

READER'S GUIDE

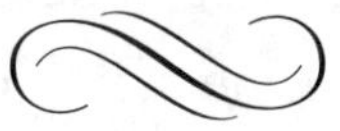

Crafting a Knockoff

BY BARBARA EMODI

1. Early in the book, Valerie explains why she loves the spring craft show: "To me, the rows of tables displaying what creative people had made over the cold, dark months were as much a confirmation of the persistence of life as the spring tulips." Are there any things that mark for you the changing of seasons or other important aspects of life?

2. Terry explains that to him, tartans are living culture, part of the past that gives roots to the future. What do you think he means by that? Can you think of anything in your own heritage that is similar? How?

3. Colleen warns her niece Valerie, "It's never a good idea to write off to malice what can be explained by accident or incompetence." Do you agree with Colleen? What does her outlook say about her personality?

4. The fashion designer Louise notes that the fashion trend she's working on is "not about the clothes; it's about the life they evoke. One with a single, clear purpose. Sustainable." How authentic do you think fashion trends are? Do you think someone's choice in fashion says anything about them?

5. In explaining to Valerie why he is back, Gilles laments, "Craftsmanship is dead. The most precious commodities these days are not things of beauty but whatever makes the most money. Authenticity is no longer valued." Do you think he is right? If so, was that his downfall, or was it due to something else?

6. In the course of the story, it is revealed that within the written records retained at Rankin's General Store "were invoices and receipts from as far back as the Depression, documenting accounts that were run up, never paid, and let go without a word, but kept among us as a record of those hard years, as a reminder of a community that had survived." What is the most meaningful written record you've seen? Was it of major historical importance or of personal significance?

7. Near the end of the story, Stuart shares that he's decided to just go along with Valerie's need for intrigue, to accept that that is who she is. To which she responds, "Might as well. That's what I've had to do." Do you have a personality trait that you've learned to accept, even though it sometimes causes you trouble? What about your partner? Have they learned to live with it, and do they themselves have a quirk that you must accept?

8. Valerie comments, "There was nothing ordinary about ordinary women … " Is that a statement you agree with? In what way are ordinary women actually extraordinary?

9. Some of the characters' motivations in this book are based on the transience of things, including fashion and technology, while other characters are more rooted in the past and tradition. Is one more powerful or important than the other? Which has more day-to-day impact?

10. Valerie comments that Gilles thinks he understands her, but he really does not understand her at all. Is that entirely true? Do you think this is a problem with people generally nowadays?

11. Near the end of the book, Valerie goes to her happy place, the store. To her, the store "spoke to me. It shared with me the memory of trees in its timbers, of bending under ocean winds and time. It told me its stories, of generation after generation of one family, one island, one place in time." Do you have a place you go when you need support or soothing?

12. Valerie explains to Stuart that the reason she cares about him, about their relationship, so much is because even though he knows her very well, she can be herself around him: "Let me tell you, if any human being can find that in another person, even once in their life, it's a miracle." Do you agree? Is this a rare occurrence, or is this common in relationships other than romantic relationships?

13. Valerie notes that the idea of using your family as a brand is new to her. Is it new to you, or can you think of other examples? Do you believe that using family as a brand is authentic? Is it a good idea?

14. A few times, Valerie observes that Heidi is often underestimated. Are there people you know, friends, family, or coworkers, whom you feel are underrated? If so, is it to the detriment of the person being underestimated or of the person selling them short?

15. Valerie explains to Stuart that although her course is about sewing knits, it's really about overcoming fear. Can you think of any activities that you've participated in that were really about something else—a class, team, or endeavor that had a separate goal than the most obvious one?

16. After walking their dogs at the school, Valerie has an opportunity to tell Stuart that she'd seen Jimmy remove the space heater, but she doesn't do so. Is that a mistake? What do you think might have happened if she had told him?

17. Valerie often makes observations about how people do things, implying that she thinks they reveal something about that person. For example, she notes that Stuart uses a fountain pen and that Catherine cuts up her pita bread while she, Valerie, tears hers. Do you agree that these sorts of things are revealing? If so, what do you use or do that you believe says something about your personality?

18. Valerie has premonitions, which she believes are hereditary in her family. Do you believe in omens, prophecy, or precognition? Are these superstitions or something real?

19. Valerie states about Stuart, "He was the first man in my life who knew who I was. This included parts of me that made him uncomfortable and made me uneasy. About myself, about him, about us." Do you believe it is necessary to share all aspects of yourself with a partner? What happens if you do or do not?

20. Several years after her return to her hometown, Valerie notes, "I felt more like the girl I had been when I was young. When a person recaptures that, they can't give it up." Do you believe it is important to feel like your younger self? Is it desirable in all cases?

21. Parts of this story focus on speed and consumption, handmade versus mass-made. Louise explains to Valerie that in fashion, "[T]he industry depends on a customer buying, again and again, year after year, whether they need the clothes or not. New is everything." Do you think that is true about industries other than fashion? Has the modern world refocused on mass production? Are there times or instances where you think this is untrue?

22. When trying to get a photo of the map, Valerie takes advantage of stereotypes. She notes, "There were advantages to being an older woman. I made a show of struggling with the camera, stabbing it with an index finger, pretending I had messed up the shot and had to try again." Do you think that people do make assumptions based on age and gender? Is that increasing or decreasing over time?

ABOUT THE AUTHOR

Barbara Emodi lives and writes in Halifax, Nova Scotia, Canada, with her husband, a rescue dog, and a cat, who all appear in her writing in various disguises. She has grown children and grandchildren in various locations and, as a result, divides her time between Halifax and the United States so no one misses her too much.

Barbara has published two sewing books—*SEW: The Garment-Making Book of Knowledge*, and *Stress-Free Sewing Solutions*, and she is a course instructor on the innovative and interactive platform Creative Spark Online Learning (by C&T Publishing). In another life, she has been a journalist, a professor, and a radio commentator.

To keep in touch with Barbara, sign up for her newsletter through her website: **babsemodi.com**

And follow her Substack column, How to Be an Older Woman for Beginners.

To keep up with Barbara, sign up for her newsletter through the link on her website. Visit Barbara online and follow on social media!

Website: babsemodi.com

Instagram: @bemodi

TikTok: @babsemodi

Fiction website: babsemodi.com

Creative Spark: creativespark.ctpub.com

Gasper's Cove Mysteries Series